VENGEANCE TO BABY VOWS

MAYA BLAKE

Recycling programs for this product may not exist in your area.

ISBN-13: 978-1-335-61403-2

Vengeance to Baby Vows

For questions and comments about the quality of this book, please contact us at CustomerService@Harlequin.com.

Harlequin Enterprises ULC
22 Adelaide St. West, 41st Floor
Toronto, Ontario M5H 4E3, Canada
www.Harlequin.com

HarperCollins Publishers
Macken House, 39/40 Mayor Street Upper,
Dublin 1, D01 C9W8, Ireland
www.HarperCollins.com

Printed in Lithuania

1 2 3 4 5 6 7 8 9 10 LIT 28 27 26 25

"You claim the child you're carrying is mine. Given that I'm choosing to believe you, you didn't think I'd want to make it right?"

"Make it right?" she echoes, laughing bitterly. "You mean lay claim. Wrap it all up in your tidy, powerful package. Control it."

I step closer. "You think I'll stand by and let my child be born without my name? Without my protection?"

"You think this child is some pawn in your inheritance game?" Her voice cuts, sharp and breathless.

I pause. Because beneath all her fury, I can see it. The hurt and the fear. The resilience holding her together like gold seams in cracked porcelain. Then I shrug. "You've presented me with a real cherry on top of a fake cake we baked together. I'm doing what needs to be done."

"I'll marry you, Ashon," Cilla says, calm and clear. "But on my terms."

My body goes taut and I thoroughly despise the feeling that too much resembles bracing myself for an unfathomable impact. Perhaps even a seismic one. I narrow my eyes. "I'm listening."

A brand-new dramatic and sizzling duet by Maya Blake!

Billionaires in the Spotlight

They're all about the lights, camera—and lots of action!

Ashon and Theo, aristocratic Ghanaian cousins, are heirs to the Biney film empire. They are the directors of their own lives, always in control. And they'll both take the lead when desire plays a part. But what happens when their passion projects go completely off script?

His one, reckless night with housekeeper Cilla is branded in Ashon's mind. Two months later, he still feels her lingering touch—and his blazing fury when she disappeared the next morning! So, when he discovers that she's pregnant, he vows to claim what's his...

Read Ashon and Cilla's story in

Vengeance to Baby Vows

Available now!

And don't miss Theo and Tessa's story

Coming soon!

Maya Blake's hopes of becoming a writer were born when she picked up her first romance at thirteen. Little did she know her dream would come true! Does she still pinch herself every now and then to make sure it's not a dream? Yes, she does! Feel free to pinch her, too, via X, Facebook or Goodreads! Happy reading!

Books by Maya Blake

Harlequin Presents

The Greek's Forgotten Marriage
Pregnant and Stolen by the Tycoon
Snowbound with the Irresistible Sicilian
Enemy's Game of Revenge
Keeping a Greek Secret

Diamonds of the Rich and Famous

Accidentally Wearing the Argentinian's Ring

A Diamond in the Rough

Greek Pregnancy Clause

Royals of Cartana

Crowned for His Son
Out of Office Nights
Snowbound and Royally Forbidden

Visit the Author Profile page
at Harlequin.com for more titles.

This one is dedicated to Idris Elba,
who was entirely responsible for this book.
Why? Because…"It's Idris" IYKYK!

CHAPTER ONE

Ashon

Bel Air, Los Angeles

If I wanted to watch someone lie to my face, I'd go back to the studio and let one of my Oscar-winning actresses give it a try. They wouldn't succeed entirely, of course, but at least they'd have the decency to fake some chemistry considering the millions I throw at them.

And hell, I might be marginally entertained while I had my time wasted.

The woman seated across from me is already sweating through her silk blouse despite the air-conditioning, blinking as if I'm holding a loaded gun instead of offering a diamond ring the size of a pigeon's egg.

'So,' I say slowly, 'you'd be my fiancée. For six months, possibly a year. We attend a few galas in Accra and around the world, stay under the same roof at my grandfather's estate, pretend to be hopelessly in love. And in return, you get half a million dollars and a very shiny piece of jewellery. All subject to complete discretion via an NDA. Are you on board with that?' Even saying the words that remind me I'm reduced to *scheming* demeans me but, alas, here we are. Rather, here *I* am. Forced to indulge in this…*farce*.

She gulps. 'You mean, you actually *want* people to believe this is real? It's not like…a script or something?'

Lord save me.

'Thank you for coming,' I say, standing. 'Have my assistant call for a car to take you…wherever you need to go.'

I don't wait for her to scurry out. Or worse, plead her hopeless case, the way I can see she's gearing up to do.

I rise and stalk to the wall of glass that frames the LA skyline, watching the lights of Sunset shimmer below me. I would punch a wall if I had any hope that the building bitterness and simmering fury would recede. That the glaring waste of my precious time in any way made the end-justifying-the-means feel any better.

It doesn't.

Fake love. Pretend devotion. Just enough performance to satisfy my grandfather's demands and unlock a legacy that should already be mine with no strings attached. One that should've been signed over to me on my thirtieth birthday if the old man wasn't, all these decades later, mired in the same mind games he seemed to think he excelled at.

I'd planned on never going back to Ghana any time soon—at least while he was alive—not even to reclaim my birthright. Until the opportunity to make a long-denied dream a reality became a siren call I couldn't resist. Even then, I'd set my sights elsewhere, far away from prying family eyes and unwanted interference.

But then Nana Biney the Third, my esteemed grandfather and a man who despised being ignored, rose as if he were a spectre I couldn't ignore. He called not to check in on his eldest grandson, or heaven forbid, to come within a blink of confessing that he'd missed me. No, that would be the epitome of weakness. The Bineys were very many things, but never, ever weak.

No, he'd called to deliver his late ultimatum in that clipped, royal tone that still managed to gut me as if I were a boy who'd disappointed him—again.

'Until you prove you're committed to legacy and family,' he'd said, 'you will not inherit the township. It will go to Theo.'

Theo.

My cousin. The poisoned clincher to end all clinchers and the one pressure point guaranteed to sting. The one thing my grandfather had known would light a fire where all else had failed.

That smug bastard could barely locate his morals, let alone manage the infrastructure of a developing film hub.

We'd grown up shoulder-to-shoulder—two alphas forever jostling for the same spotlight—but our visions had diverged as if split railway lines.

Theodore Biney, all Savile Row polish and architectural swagger, who'd once turned a boutique hotel in Lisbon into a gaudy money pit just to impress a super-model investor. He loves projects that make headlines as much as he loves the blueprints themselves. He can sketch a gravity-defying hotel at breakfast and negotiate its funding by lunch. What he can't resist is turning every triumph into a monument to Theodore. Hand him Obibini's land and I know he'll chase dazzling towers first, community storytelling second.

The prospect of surrendering my father's dream to a cousin who'd rather win the world's gaze than nurture its voices knots my stomach. Which is exactly why I'm standing here, plotting the perfect fiancée, the perfect performance. A future Nana can't veto, because I'll bend every Hollywood contact before I let Theodore Biney's ego become the face of Africa's first world-class studio.

The enclave—Nkyinkyim—was everything I'd been

building towards. A chance to bring African storytelling to life. A pipe dream realised against all odds and creating real, much-needed jobs. Opportunity. Pride. A long-denied voice on the global stage.

Hunting for a real fiancée—the tabloids would feast—had been a non-starter, of course. Not after my last attempt at a relationship had hit the skids faster than a stunt car on a rain-soaked backlot.

Delphine had shown me very quickly how false affection turns to dollar signs. The moment our involvement hit Page Six, her lawyers hit me with a revised NDA and a clause for 'image-maintenance payments'.

She'd loved my studio clout and billions a whole lot more than my admittedly tough to crack heart, and when I pulled the plug on our liaison she'd barely waited till sunset before she'd sold the break-up story for six figures.

Intimacy, legacy and fortune mix as if oil and acid. I'm not offering a real-life liaison—and access to half my net worth—to another heartless opportunist. That lesson has been well-learned.

A fake fiancée I can control, along with a scripted romance I can exit. *That* is what will aid in achieving my ultimate goal.

Messy and patently false feelings won't blindside me if I know from day one they're not part of the contract.

My grandfather, with one phone call filled with oiled threats and blatant manipulation, had boiled down years of hard work, pride swallowing, strategy and counter-strategy to whether *I was in love*. Or worse, whether I intended to procreate.

And based on the answer I'd needed to provide during that dreadful conversation, everything I'd worked for would all go to hell unless I produced a woman. A partner. A showpiece of tradition and affection. Someone Nana Biney would deem 'suitable'.

So here I am, reduced to scrambling for talent to stage the most important role in my life.

Fake it until I make it.

Whirling from the window, I drop behind my desk, lean back in the leather chair, fingers steepled, gaze fixed on the next hopeful young actress sat across from me.

She's all gloss and curated charm, every movement precise—her smile, her beautiful dark chocolate skin, her laughter, even the way she crosses her legs as if in First Lady poise.

And yet...*she's not real enough to fool a Biney, never mind Nana Biney himself.*

No, most definitely not *him*. The man who spent decades standing at the shoulders of presidents and prime ministers, whispering pearls of wisdom none dared ignore.

He'd earned himself royalty status from that. A status he'd passed down, with very many strings attached, to his progeny. Strings he wielded like the master puppeteer he is.

'I can be whatever you need me to be,' the actress purrs, voice syrupy with promise. Sweet to the point of sickly. 'A wife. A girlfriend. A mistress. A who—'

I lift my hand and offer a tight smile to stop this debacle before it goes any further. She would be lucky to utter a single word in my grandfather's presence before he had her thrown out. Like they always do, she gears up to plead her case. I glance at my assistant, Renée, who springs into action from the corner of the room.

'Thank you. We'll be in touch,' Renée says briskly.

The actress leaves, hips swaying as if she's still auditioning.

The moment the door shuts, I scrub a hand down my face. 'This is a waste of time.'

'Well,' Renée says without looking up from her iPad, 'your impatience aside, it's still the perfect solution to your problems. You want your inheritance and your production house. Your grandfather wants to see you settled. In love. Or at the very least committed-adjacent. A small price to pay if you ask me.'

I swallow the growl building in my throat, the utter loathing of the trap closing in on me. 'I'd rather jump off a bridge.'

Renée arches a brow. 'There's always option B. Forget the studio deal and let Nana B gloat from his ancestral throne while he parcels your birthright to this cousin to build his questionable monument.'

I glare at her poorly disguised reverse psychology. She's not wrong. That's the worst part. My grandfather would carry through with his threat without a second thought. Many had called his bluff in the past and lived to regret it. And it stuck deep in my craw that he'd found the perfect counter to my next move—to block my every contingency, at least on the African continent for as long as he lived.

I already tried to circumvent him once and been summoned to see Nana's lawyers who'd made it clear.

The Biney Trust would tangle me up in court for years before he released the land or the substantial thirty-year endowment funding that came with it—the funds I needed for my legacy project, *Obibini Studios*. I'd been firmly told that unless I publicly 'demonstrated stability and commitment worthy of the family name' any attempts to fund a similar project elsewhere would not succeed.

Their words. Not mine. As if I needed a surround sound echo of my grandfather's words. As if their collective voices didn't boil down to 'find a woman'. Fast.

That's your best and only short-term option.

The underlying message beneath the insult is even louder.

Because as important as you think you are, you'll never be enough on your own.

And that?

That's the fucking knife in my gut.

Forty-eight hours later and my patience is a fraction of paper-thin.

I've interviewed models, actresses, even a minor royal. The next few candidates blur together—Instagram-famous, fashion-forward, all airbrushed perfection and zero soul. Hell, it's almost as if they've taken a leaf out of Delphine's book to be all polish and no substance. I stifle a bark of acid laughter to think perhaps they've done *exactly* that. Delphine's exit was deliberate, loud and extremely *public* after all.

Renée tries her best to keep things professional, but even she's yawning by the fifth 'I believe in true love' and 'I'm the perfect candidate for you' monologues.

'I swear,' I mutter after the sixth exit, 'if one more of them says she'd die for me, I'll test it.'

Renée laughs…until my deadly serious face causes her humour to whittle away. 'You've been in Hollywood too long. You forget the art of subtle lies.'

I lean forward, elbows on my knees, making an effort to unclench my jaw and release my bitterness for a moment so I can just…breathe. Telling subtle lies is one thing, but seeing—to a single one of these candidates—the glint in their eyes when they scan the academy award trophies behind me, and the naked ambition beyond the role I'm offering, has bile crawling up my throat. Maybe that's my problem—the inability to divorce myself from the disaster to end all disasters labelled Delphine.

'I built a damn empire from nothing. Sold my first script on spec. Got *Variety*'s "One to Watch" before I turned thirty. But none of that means anything to him.'

Renée pauses for a moment, then sighs. Approaching the chair just vacated by the last candidate, she sits down. I know what's coming and, unlike many subordinates, she's not shy about voicing her opinion. As my oldest and most loyal employee, in a world based on fleeting connections and make-believe, she's earned her right to speak her mind. Even when I don't want to hear it.

'He's old school. Ghanaian royalty wrapped in brocade and power and entitlement. No one has said no to him in decades. But…is there a reason to think he's just adding strings on a project he wants to make happen, too?'

'No,' I say bitterly. 'He's disappointed. Always has been. I chose stories over steel mills. Lights over cocoa farms. Every trip home he reminded me that I'd let him down.' Memory sears harder. 'He called my work childish. Fiction. Weak.'

Renée closes her iPad, sensing the crack beneath the surface.

'You don't want to go back,' she says gently.

'No.' I stand, jaw tight. 'Not like this and not under his say-so. Because every time I do, he tries to remind me that I'm still that boy in the guest wing—an heir in name only. Never enough. I despise that he's forcing my hand. Using what matters most.'

Obibini Studios is my vision of African cinema, told without apology or foreign filters. Ghanaian stories, Ghanaian talent, shot on our soil with global scale.

It's everything I hadn't dared to dream of as a boy. A reality within the palm of my hand.

And it's hanging on the illusion of a relationship I don't want, with a woman I'm paying to play a role and therefore can't trust as far as I can throw her. All for the approval of a master manipulator I no longer respect.

A growl escapes before I can stop it.

Renée checks the list, ever the assistant eager for forward momentum. 'We've got two more tomorrow. One of them is a model-slash-activist. The other's a tech heiress who's been to rehab, but she's clean now. She's been to Ghana a few times during Detty December. Loves it there. She might just swing it for you.'

I grunt, doubting *that*. Dirty or 'Detty' December has become the catchphrase for the near hedonism in Accra and the surrounding cities. As much as I loved the tourism and cultural boom it'd brought to the country, I doubt a woman fresh from rehab was the right person to plunge into an atmosphere like that.

Still, I look up when a glass slides across my desk. It's filled with two shots of my favourite cognac. 'Is this sympathy or a preamble to more bad news,' I gripe.

Renée grimaces at my arid tone. 'It's a don't-bite-my-head-off-but…'

'But what?'

'But unless you want to start taking out your own trash and cooking your own meals, you need to pick a name from the list of housekeepers I sent you on Monday.'

Did I despise the fresh grip of tension that seized my middle? Very, very much. 'Remind me again why I pay several agencies and minions to handle this and yet you're bothering me with this?'

Renée rolls her eyes. Heaven bless her for being old enough to be my mother, therefore necessitating my ingrained imperative—as a well-brought up Biney of the Great Ghana Bineys—to treat her with the utmost respect.

'Because you said something about not wanting another Cilla on your hands.'

A brand-new sensation, dirty and shaming, rises to join the tension. Sadly, I *did* say those words. But out of a healthy dose of self-loathing. And yes, a respectable amount of bitterness and chagrin too.

Because didn't I swear heaven and earth against another Delphine, only to end up with a stealthier, more cunning version? One with sensible shoes and a seemingly genuine smile who'd found a chink I would've sworn wasn't present until she'd exposed it.

So yes, it was true I didn't want another one of *her* to ever cross my threshold. I live in a town where gold-digging was birthed. You would think I'd have that reminder emblazoned on my forehead or something.

And yet Cilla Rockson, the housekeeper who once moved as if shadows across my Bel Air mansion, her eyes always a fraction too sharp, too aware—had proved she had a talent for living up to the label. I'd suspected it. Succeeded in avoiding it.

Until the night my world burned to ash, and I reached for her as a drowning man would a life jacket. Except it'd been a jacket riddled with holes and subterfuge.

We had one night. One reckless, unforgettable night. The kind of sex not even the best director in the world could replicate on the silver screen. The kind that made even cynical poets scrounge up a meaningful line or sonnet. All. Fucking. Lies.

I drifted into a half-dream afterward, drowsy with grief and sated with sex, only to wake before dawn to a cool bed and the kind of foreboding that guaranteed box office. I'd found her, drawn by the sound of papers rustling. There'd she'd been, her hair still wild from my fingers, standing in my private study, phone light glinting as she hovered over documents she'd had no business looking at.

'Couldn't sleep,' she'd said when I appeared in the doorway, forcing a smile. 'Thought I'd tidy.' The story was flimsy, but I swallowed it, tugged her back to bed, convinced myself paranoia would ruin the memory faster than truth. Yet my gut snarled. Continued to snarl until a deeper background check had revealed that indeed, a UCLA dual-degree talent like she possessed doesn't spend six months scrubbing marble for minimum wage unless she's mining something more valuable.

At sunrise she was gone, her uniform returned, a terse resignation letter on a kitchen napkin. Security footage confirmed the punch in my stomach. She'd snapped photos of my private documents about Obibini Studios the moment she thought I was out cold.

So I did what every Biney heir is taught—erase the threat before it spreads. I told myself it was just protocol, that the woman who polished my floors had played me. But no amount of blacklisting has erased the truth that haunts every night since—it wasn't a lapse in judgement. And dammit, it was also the most visceral connection I've ever experienced, aided no doubt by the weight of my grief, but nevertheless...a connection that still caught me hard and raw when I allowed myself to dwell on it. Which I absolutely wasn't going to keep doing now.

Did it grate that she'd quit before I could locate the words to fire her? Sure.

I'd convinced myself it was for the best. That anyone that over-qualified didn't scrub toilets for the view. But I'd devoted too much time developing a reasons for that ploy.

All very, very unsavoury.

I drain my glass, every intention of washing her memory down with my next swallow. But then it happens—soft, sneaky. A flicker of memory. Dark curls. Full lips. Thick hips. About as far from the stick-thin imitations who strut down Rodeo Drive as you could get.

That single night branded me more than I ever admitted. The sound of my name leaving her mouth in a seductive plead. The false promise of comfort and succour in her eyes.

Cilla.

Turns out she was the best actress never to audition for a role I wasn't offering.

The best actress…

Yesu. I freeze for a moment as possibilities clang like church bells. If she was playing a role then, could she—

I'm already standing. Already brushing past Renée, who calls my name in confusion.

I head for the elevator, phone in hand. By the time I'm striding into the underground garage, I'm already dialling.

'Get me an address,' I say to my security chief. 'Cilla Rockson. Need it in the next fifteen minutes. Everything else you can dig up should be forwarded to me by six a.m. tomorrow.'

I kill the call and climb into my car, heart pounding harder than it should. Because maybe I don't know what I'm doing. I need someone to lie for me. Pretend to love me. Let the world believe we were meant to be.

And there's only one woman who ever made it feel true for a few short hours shrouded in grief and lust.

Maybe I'm playing with something I can't afford to feel. But I'm going to see her anyway.

And this time, I won't be the one left wanting.

Hell, I might find some much needed satisfaction before this repulsive demand is over.

Cilla

The knock on my door comes just after eleven p.m.

In this sketchy part of town I've been forced to make my

home, it's either a drug dealer or trouble in a suit. I'm not sure which I'd prefer.

I glance through the peephole as any responsible, albeit reluctant Angelino would if they don't want to be robbed or worse, then jerk back, my heart leaping into my throat.

For endless seconds I stare blankly at the worn wood. Then because it's stupidly late and I can't risk my neighbours' stream of vitriol, I yank open the door of my shabby apartment in Koreatown, and stare straight into the eyes of a cruel monster.

My heart does this stupid lurch thing. Then fury punches through the surprise.

'What the hell do you want?'

Ashon Biney stands in my doorway as if he owns the goddamn building. Which, knowing his sheer filthy rich status, his shrewd head for business, and that single-minded, almost borderline feral need for independence and to own and control everything around him, he probably does.

Perfect suit. Perfect jaw. Toffee-brown eyes that used to look through me, the hired help, as if I didn't exist—until that night he was drowning and I made the mistake of saving him.

Now, two long and harrowing months later, he's here.

My ex-boss.

My one-night stand.

My biggest mistake.

'You look…' he starts, eyes sweeping over me in that infuriatingly male way that makes me want to slam the door. *Before* he steals all the air from my lungs.

'Poor?' I offer scathingly. 'Because I am.'

My words bounce off his mile-wide shoulders but there's the minutest flare of his nostrils before complete control is regained. 'Funny,' Ashon says, eyes narrowing. 'Last I checked, students who graduate top of their film cohort and land a

Sundance shortlist aren't usually scraping by as housekeepers. I should ask why you're wasting a sabbatical on my dust bunnies.' He snaps his fingers. 'Oh wait, I *would've* asked you this two months ago, except you ran away before I got the chance.'

My insides go hot, then cold but I fight to retain my composure. Showing guilt or any other human emotion around this man is like leaking blood in shark-infested water and expecting not to be ripped to shreds. So what if my shoddy attempt at playing detective had gone woefully awry?

Ashon Biney and the mighty Biney clan as a whole were still responsible for the heinous wrong against my family. A wrong I haven't given up on righting.

'Because sometimes magic costs money before it makes money,' I shoot back the part truth, hoping it would distract him from the real reason I'd chosen to scrub his floors. 'Freelance documentaries don't pay LA rent. And a sabbatical cleaning Bel-Air mansions got me closer to the gatekeepers I needed—starting with you.'

Let him think it was a professional leg up that I wanted. It's much better for him not to know the full truth. Although the prospects of uncovering *that* truth now he'd made sure I've been blacklisted…

I shake my head as his head tilts.

'I wasn't born yesterday, Miss Rockson. You could've been in Venice winning Best Documentary but you chose to infiltrate my house ostensibly to alphabetise my spice rack. Either your career counsellor's a sadist or you were running a long con.'

Shockingly, he doesn't seem to care either way. Why am I surprised? He's a Biney. Therefore he's *that* arrogant. That untouchable.

He continued, 'But since I suspect what your end goal is, I'm here to make you an offer.'

'Indulge me.' I strive for boredom and silently pat myself on the back for skimming close enough. 'What do you think my end goal was?'

Shrewd eyes bore into me for a weighted second. 'Money of course. Something salacious to tell to TMZ?' A sharp, devastating smile. 'I'm well-versed in what freelance documentarians earn. Just as I'm an expert on how gold-diggers operate.'

Curiosity bites with the last one—especially with the extra acid in his tone—but I force a laugh, one part incredulous, two parts bitter. 'Oh, I've heard this one before. What will it cost me, besides being blacklisted from every other meaningful job in the city?'

His jaw tightens. Just slightly. Most people wouldn't notice. I do.

Because I used to clean his cufflinks. Wash his sheets. Bring his mother's portrait fresh flowers every Sunday as if some loyal, invisible ghost.

I know his silences. I know what it means when he watches with narrowed eyes and speaks *too* calmly. Often it's the scant minute before minions flee, most pale as ghosts, some never to be seen again.

'I didn't blacklist you.'

I snort. 'Really? Because after I quit, suddenly all those nice promises of re-hiring turned to radio silence. I've got receipts, Ashon. Your people told my would-be employers I was "emotionally unstable". That I "breached confidential conduct". That I was *unreliable*.'

He doesn't deny it. Doesn't even blink.

'Because we both know you were doing more than cleaning in my study that night you left,' he says instead, voice cool.

Dismissive. 'Without notice I might add. Tell me what that is if it isn't the act of the guilty. Oh and *after* sneaking into my bed like it was your reward for a promotion you never earned.'

Rage blooms as if wildfire in my chest.

'Sneak?' I hiss. 'You arrogant son of a—*you* pulled *me* in that night. You said all those…hot things to me. You kissed *me*. You went from barely noticing I existed to being all over me. Did you seriously think I was going to wait around for the cringing morning after routine? Did you forget I'd been around enough to watch you roll out the exit carpet for more than one sad sister who made the mistake of succumbing to men like you? So no, that wasn't cowardice or whatever label you want to hang on it. That was self-respect.'

A beat of silence stretches between us, tight as a violin string.

I see it then—his gaze shifting. Not softening. Just recalibrating. As if I've reminded him I have teeth.

Good.

Let him remember I'm not that quiet housekeeper who used to pick up his broken whiskey glasses and apologise when he stormed and prowled and barked at others. *Except he hadn't done that that night. He'd been almost* human... *downed by grief and cloaked in the loneliness you couldn't resist comforting.*

I'm barefoot, wearing an old tank top with a bleach stain and cotton shorts that sag at the waistband, but I fold my arms and hold my chin high. If I'm going down, I'm going down proud. 'Why are you here, Ashon?'

He hesitates for the first time since I opened the door, and I wonder if he's going to demand I call him Mr Biney or Sir as everyone except his assistant is supposed to. I wonder if the punch of inappropriately pleased surprise at that invitation to call him Ashon when we first met would be equal to the punch of disappointment if he reversed that invitation.

But his eyes merely flick over my shoulder, taking in the sad excuse for a hallway behind me. Exposed pipes. Peeling paint. A chipped mirror I picked up for five bucks at a yard sale in a wild bid for cheer amidst a daunting but necessary undertaking for justice. Even if that undertaking involved lowering myself to cleaning this man's floors while temporarily abandoning the work I loved.

Then he looks back at me.

And something flashes behind his gaze—disgust, maybe. Or pity. Either one makes me want to spit.

'You should eat,' he says, out of nowhere. 'You look…thin.'

'I'm not your problem. Never was, never will be.'

He presses his lips together. Exhales once. Then, infuriatingly, steps past me into the apartment without asking.

I whirl around. 'What the hell—?'

But he's already inside, scanning the tiny space as if it's a crime scene. Or the perfect hovel for one of his characters to do deplorable things in.

My one-room apartment smells like microwaved plantains and desperation. A single rickety fan turns in the corner. My laptop sits on the chipped coffee table, surrounded by sticky notes of possible jobs to explore and an empty bottle of hibiscus soda. A folded blanket serves as my couch pillow.

Ashon takes it all in with the sharp-eyed precision of a man trained to assess the value of a thing before touching it.

His face doesn't change. But I see it. The judgement. The shock.

And beneath that? Something worse.

Regret.

As if maybe he didn't expect me to fall this far? As if

this isn't a reflection of how hard I've fought, but how far I must've deserved to fall.

My spine stiffens and I summon the pride of my ancestors. The very people he and his family wronged. The very reason I ever stepped into Ashon Biney's orbit in the first place. 'If you came here to gloat, you should leave now. Before I call the cops,' I snarl. Thank God my voice emerges strong and steady despite the pathetic quaking inside.

Dark eyes return to me. Skate over me and lingering in places he has no right to. Before, 'No. I did not.'

'Then what? To rub salt in the wounds you made?'

'Believe it or not, I came to make you an offer.'

I laugh again—low, caustic, my nails biting into my flesh. Because for a moment, my mind leaps where it's absolutely not supposed to. Back to thousand thread-count sheets, hot words whispered in the dark while hotter bodies writhed. 'Oh, you want a repeat performance?'

His eyes flick to mine. Something there burns, but he hides it fast. After another quick circuit with an infinitesimal pause at my hips. Hips that were much fuller this time two months ago. Hips he gripped and held on as if his life depended on—

'No, Miss Rockson. As you astutely observed, I'm not one to revisit old scripts,' he says, briskly. 'This is strictly business.'

'Right,' I say, folding my arms tighter, to hold in the stupid sting of his words. 'Because you're all about boundaries.'

He ignores the jab. Walks to the window. Stares out at the flickering Koreatown skyline as if he's considering how far he's fallen just by being here in my grimy space.

'My grandfather wants me to settle down. Publicly. Formally. He's threatening to withhold something important that I need until I do.'

I blink. Recalibrating too because this…wasn't what I expected. 'And this concerns me why?' I bite out eventually.

His chin rises, as if he needs to rise above his own words. 'I need a fake wife.'

'You need a fake wife,' I echo flatly.

'Hmm. A temporary one. Just for a year, maybe two. Long enough to satisfy the board, the media and the old man.'

'And you thought of me?' My voice is still flat. Because he's still making zero sense.

'Eventually.'

That too stings more than it should.

'Oh right. Your A-list friends and minions are too busy polishing their imaginary academy awards so you're scraping the barrel now. FYI, Mr Hotshot Producer Director, I'm not some pawn for you to use when you've run out of respectable options.' I point to the door, hating that my fingers shake and that my insides wrench as if they have been tossed into a tumble dryer.

'No,' he agrees. 'But you're the one who fled my bed and my house with some flimsy excuse about impropriety. Or am I misquoting that napkin resignation?'

'Because I had *dignity*.'

He turns then, fully. Slowly. And the temperature in the room shifts.

The man standing in my apartment isn't the same one I used to work for. He's harder now. Meaner. Hungrier. A predator long-starved shown the feast he intends to devour. Come hell or high water.

'Cilla,' he says softly, dangerously, 'you made a choice that night. Don't pretend you didn't know what it would cost you.'

'I didn't expect *you* to burn down the rest of my chances because we had sex and you never got your chance to throw me out before I exited. Or are you going to stand there and tell me you wanted something…*more.*' I emphasise the word, throw in a thick slice of sarcasm. And completely ignore my clenched gut.

His jaw flexes. Several beats pass in silence.

'Yeah, that's what I thought. And, God, even if I did make a choice,' I finish, 'here you are. Asking me to crawl back into your world like nothing happened. Is your ego that obscenely huge or are you just heartless?'

'Neither,' he says, then shrugs. 'Both. What I think or feel shouldn't feature in this. I'm asking you to walk in with your head held high. By my side for a finite time. I'll pay you well, fatten that bank account you so obviously need fattening. We'll set clear rules. A timeline of one year. If you're that attached to cleaning other people's dirty floors, I'll ensure you get your name cleared. Hell, I'll write you a personal recommendation if you want. Or,' he stops, purely for dramatic effect I'm sure, then shrugs, 'if you do a good enough job, I might even put in a word to put you back on track for your true, *honest* calling.'

My honest calling. Film. Documentary-creating. A career I've missed more than I thought I would. But then I'm reminded who I'm dealing with. A ruthless predator born of a pride of predators.

My laugh is shaky, bitter. 'What could be this important to you that you would lower yourself to this. To me?'

His jaw works for several seconds. 'It's a family trust's release for my studio.'

Of course it is. Only a few key people knew of Ashon's plans. But I'd been his housekeeper once upon a time. Heard the phone calls, the excitement. Knew how important this was to him. Important enough to ignore the small matter of the family he's wronged on the short road to achieving yet another celestial dream, uncaring of the anguish and heartache left in his wake. 'And all I have to do is smile at your side and pretend I'm the lucky one.' My tone is mocking.

His voice is equally low and mocking. 'You'd rather stay here, eating ramen and despair?'

The silence that follows is deafening. With every atom of my being I want to shout that yes, I want to stay here. Yes, I want to keep my pride.

But also no.

Because I'm tired. And broke. And bleeding behind the smile I wear when I go interview for jobs that never call me back. *Because of him.*

I meet his eyes. A quiver of...something slides through me. I might have burned my opportunity once by making the worst decision of my life. But maybe this was my second chance to right wrongs that still churn my insides. A chance to come at this from another angle? Surely being inside the Biney circle again will be the perfect opportunity to thread my way to the proof no lawyer has unearthed, the key to reclaiming everything they stripped from my family.

I suck in an unsteady breath as a part of me recoils. Because stepping back into Ashon's electric orbit means steady exposure to the man who short-circuits every sensible thought I've ever owned. The reminder that he'd only needed to walk into a room in his Bel-Air mansion for me to grow breathless and throbbing in private places is a cringe-worthy, pulse-tripping one I don't want or need.

And yet, if there ever was a sign from the cosmos or the ancestors that I couldn't...*shouldn't* ignore...isn't it this one, beating an urgent tattoo beneath my ribs?

'I want three months' pay up front,' I blurt before the decision has even hardened in my mind. Then, for the hell of it, I go for broke. 'I want my reputation restored, publicly. And I want a contract that gives me control over how this ends.'

His mouth curves. Not quite a smile. Something sharper. Calculating. 'I knew you'd come to the table eventually. But you should learn better negotiating tactics. Definitely better than asking for three months' pay. I'll give you what I offered everyone I auditioned for the role. Half a million dollars on you signing an agreement. But I have clauses of my own. Some non-negotiable.'

The churning intensifies. I swallow, attempt not to show hostility or how boggled I am by the money he's offering. 'Which are?'

'They include, but not limited to, physical contact that is staged well enough to satisfy the world's worst cynic, who just happens to be my grandfather. Which means you'll need to work on that loathsome expression on your face, for starters.' His gaze trails over me once more, lingering in places I don't want it to. Hating the tiny little fires he leaves behind. 'A wardrobe upgrade. My lawyer will provide a fuller list by morning.'

I don't flinch. I won't give him the satisfaction.

'Don't worry. I'll hold my own without holding my nose, Mr Biney. But when this ends,' I say coolly, 'you don't get to touch me. Ever again.'

His eyes flare, blaze with mockery. Then he nods. 'Agreed.'

But I see the lie behind his eyes. The same one pulsing beneath my skin.

Because the thing between us isn't dead. It's just waiting to burn us both alive.

And maybe I'll let it.

Because Ashon Biney thinks he's playing me. Thinks I'm some desperate woman too proud to admit she needs him. Or worse, a woman he can order about to suit his needs.

But he doesn't know everything. He doesn't know why I took that housekeeping job in the first place. Doesn't know how long I searched for a way into his orbit. Into the records his family buried generations ago.

He doesn't know about the land.

My land.

The same plot his grandfather snatched up after my father defaulted on a predatory loan and tossed in with his precious enclave. The one that should've been part of my inheritance, part of my future. The land my mother begged him not to take when we were drowning in debt.

It isn't just acreage on a survey map. It's the mango grove where my cousins and I hunted fireflies, the clay riverbank where my grandmother taught me the rhythm of clothes-washing by hand, the ridge where my father carved our initials into the trunk of an ancient Odum tree and promised every harvest would pay my school fees. I still smell the cocoa blossoms when I close my eyes. I still hear my father coughing, begging Nana Biney's lawyer to spare us.

Ashon doesn't know that I grew up hearing his family's name as a curse. That I swore one day I'd get it back. Working in his house was supposed to be my way in. I'd planned to stay quiet, stay useful, keep my head down until I found the documents.

The proof. The leverage.

Instead, I fell into his bed and lost the one thing I couldn't afford to gamble—his oblivious trust. It all backfired. A flash of a lethal smile and a display of humanity was all it took to shatter my defences. To succumb to dark chemistry and intoxicating sex.

Then, realising my mistake, I ran. And he responded the way powerful men shouldn't but repeatedly choose to. Ashon Biney erased me.

But now he's here. With a fake contract. A desperate gambit. A seat beside him at the table.

He thinks he's dragging me into his game. But what he doesn't see is that he's just invited me back into the house.

And this time, I won't leave empty-handed.

He sears me with one last look before he heads to the door. 'Things will move quickly. Renée, my assistant will be in touch first thing in the morning, with an itinerary. But I suggest you pack to travel in the next twenty-four hours.'

I trail after him, hating the dominance of his masculine scent in my space. In my shabby sanctuary. Hating that I can't look away from him for more than one damn second. 'One last thing.'

He stiffens. Turns. 'Let me guess—the fee I offered suddenly feels light? You want double? Or triple?'

Typical Biney. I let a slow sneer curl. 'Hold on to your wallet. But remember, you came to me, which makes us partners, not master and pawn. Keep that in mind before you attempt a trademark bait-and-switch.'

His brow lifts, intrigued, annoyed. 'As unsavoury as that sounds, what exactly will you do to me?'

I step closer, voice sweet as syrup, sharp as glass. 'I'll remind you why you should've stayed in your side of town, Mr Biney.'

CHAPTER TWO

Ashon

The first time I kissed her, she tasted like defiance. Like something I had no business wanting, something stamped with red flags but couldn't help taking.

I hadn't planned it. Hell, she'd factored *nowhere* on my agenda.

I came home far less drunk than I wanted to be, far angrier than the occasion demanded, ruined in a tuxedo that still stank of funeral lilies. Nana's voice had echoed in my skull all night—*you've lost touch with who you are, Ashon. You've lost your honour and, the way you're going, you'll lose your bloodline too. I hope this little pipedream of yours will be worth it in the long run.*

Doors slamming behind me as if I could shut him out, frustrated growls building, I stumbled into my kitchen at midnight, yanked off my tie and there she was.

Ćilla. Barefoot with a messy bun and an apron and far too sexy temptation for a man on his last nerve could withstand. Washing a pan like it had offended her ancestors.

'You're not supposed to be here,' she'd said without looking at me.

I dropped the whiskey bottle I'd snagged on my way in onto the counter and ignored her. Until she turned.

Until those dark eyes pinned me with something sharp and electric. Read every expression I hadn't bothered to camouflage because, damn it, I was in my house. My space. And she had no right to be there but there she was, nevertheless.

'You were at the funeral,' she said softly. 'How was it?'

My voice came out raw. 'My father's gone. And now so's my mother. That's how it was.' Because Nana hadn't even waited until my father, the man who'd effectively placed himself as a buffer between son and grandson, my last champion in a sea of sceptics, was in the ground before he'd sharpened his barbs.

Cilla didn't utter the catch-all sorry for your loss. Nor did she give me pity.

She just walked over, took the freshly poured glass from my hand and poured a drop on the floor with the usual muttered incantation to the ancestors for my mother's safe passage to the afterlife, then poured the rest down the drain.

'Drink water, Ashon,' she murmured, her breath brushing my jaw. 'And go to bed. You'll thank me in the morning.'

I didn't heed that unwanted advice on top of the unwanted pile I'd received all day. I caught her to me, pinned her insolent little waist and that plump ass that had teased and taunted me for *weeks* against the kitchen island.

And I kissed her instead.

Cilla

Ashon moves through the narrow aisle of the jet like he owns the sky itself. All long limbs and quiet power, dressed in slate-grey slacks, jacket and a black shirt rolled at the sleeves. He shouldn't still have this effect on me, not after everything, but God help me—he does.

His skin is a warm, golden-brown blend of sun and shadow,

the legacy of his Ghanaian father and American mother etched into every angle of his face. High cheekbones, strong jawline, and a mouth that looks carved for sin and scorn in equal measure. The tight, dark curls of his hair coils against his scalp in a way that makes my fingers itch with memory.

And then there are his eyes. Dark and unreadable and far too shrewd. Bottomless wells of calculation and heat and everything that's made him a seemingly overnight success in Hollywood with blockbuster after masterpiece after blockbuster.

As he glances at me once across the width of the plane and plush seats, my breath snags, because buried under all that arrogance is the man I shouldn't still want.

The one who once touched me like I was something essential he desperately needed.

The one who now looks at me like I might be a threat to everything he's built.

And maybe I am. I'm guessing we'll find out sooner rather than later.

I take a breath and drag my gaze—far too taxingly—from him to take in my surroundings once again, attempting not to display the awe trawling through me.

The Biney jet is obscenely luxurious.

Cream leather seats, polished mahogany accents, a flight attendant who looks like she was plucked from a beauty pageant.

I sink into the buttery seat and try not to flinch when Ashon sits across from me, his knees almost brushing mine. The hum of the engines starts the second his seat belt clicks into place, like some carefully orchestrated synchrony.

In minutes we lift off and Los Angeles fades behind us.

Ahead lies Ghana. A hidden or ignored tangled history, and a man who makes my pulse race for all the wrong reasons.

Ashon's assistant, a woman named Renée, had swept into my life like a hurricane within hours of my agreement. Motherly in her tone, but sharp as cut glass beneath the warmth, she'd handled the logistics of my transformation with unnerving efficiency. Garment bags had appeared at my door like offerings to a reluctant queen. Spa appointments were booked before I could blink. Personal stylists descended, nodding at my figure and discussing neckline theory like I wasn't in the room.

Now, sitting across from him, I'm wrapped in a form-fitting silk blouse the color of obsidian, tucked into high-waisted cream trousers that hug me in all the places a woman is supposed to look expensive. My braids are swept into a soft crown. Gold hoops catch the cabin lights when I turn my head.

I look like someone who belongs in a private jet.

But I don't feel like me. At all. Not since Ashon's assistant had arrived on my doorstep, iPad in hand, clipped orders at the ready.

I'd seen Renée once or twice in person. The first time, she'd looked me up and down with a gentle, assessing gaze that had no business being so perceptive. Something in her expression—withheld judgement but not disapproval exactly—had made my skin itch. It was almost like she *knew*. Like she'd guessed I hadn't taken the housekeeper job out of pure financial need. That I'd entered Ashon's world looking for something more.

If she did know, she hadn't said a word.

The lawyers had been worse. All charm until it came time to write the terms. Then it was masks off—ruthless, clinical precision. Every clause a veiled threat and every signature a show of force and surrender. I signed because I had to. Because backing out would've cost more than my pride.

But facing the full force of Ashon Biney's machine—his

wealth, his reach, his absolute control—had been sobering. A reminder that he owns more than companies and mansions.

He owns *narratives*.

And I just stepped into one of them. Possibly the most important one of his life.

I want to reassure myself that high risk means high reward, or even *just* reward, and more importantly, reparations for me and my family.

But… I can't shake the ominous notion that's continued to grip me since he turned up on my doorstep last night.

That this might cost me more than I anticipate paying.

He unbuttons his jacket and leans back like he does this every other Tuesday. Which he probably does. 'We should talk,' he says.

'I assumed we'd already done that through our lawyers and your assistant,' I reply, keeping my voice breezy and not at all tart like my insides feel.

But he's in business mode now, eyes sharp and assessing. 'We need to get our story straight. Dates. Places. Details. My grandfather doesn't play. He'll look into every corner of your life.'

'Charming.' My dry tone is totally undermined by my shaking hand as I reach for my glass and take an unnecessary sip of mineral water.

'He's old-school and very…thorough.'

I glance at the champagne bucket someone placed beside me. The flutes waiting for a celebration. Or just par for the cause because this is how the other half live. I haven't touched it. Too dangerous. Drink and unstable emotions were what brought me to this in the first place.

'What do you need to know?' I ask.

Ashon taps his fingers against the armrest. 'Let's start with how we met. What drew me to you. What made us fall…as it were,' he says drily. A complete opposite to the way his dark brown eyes drill into me.

That word. *Fall.* My chest goes tight. Even as my brain shrieks, *as if.*

'Maybe don't oversell it,' I say, forcing a smirk. 'We both know I was your housekeeper. You were emotionally compromised. One night doesn't exactly scream epic love.'

He leans forward, eyes dark. 'It might not have screamed it. But it felt real. Until it didn't.'

That shuts me up. The air between us thickens.

Until he adds, 'We'll go with that. The first part, at least. Sometimes the simplest moments are the most profound. Not every love story is a *coup de foudre*.'

It feels impossible for relief to co-exist with hurt. For both to sit on a foundation of apprehension. And yet… 'Okay,' I say, shifting. 'How about this? I was your housekeeper, my contract ended, but we reconnected by chance. You ran into me at some grocery store in West Hollywood, pushing a cart full of ramen and peanut butter.'

He huffs a sardonic laugh. 'That would sound…plausible *if* I did my own shopping.'

I shrug. 'You could pretend you're less of an A-hole who barks at minions for not colour-coding his green juices with the days of the week. Turned over a new, better leaf for the sake of saving your soul before it's too late?' My tongue is firmly in my cheek.

His nostrils flare but his eyes remain quirked. And I swear I catch the faintest hint of amusement before he kills it.

'So we met at the grocery store. I told you to go to hell. Which, again, tracks. Because I'm wishing that right now.'

He studies me, my words bouncing ineffectually off his broad shoulders. 'And then?'

'And then you wore me down. With your influence. And whispered promises. And your absurd jawline.'

His mouth lifts, just slightly. But it's not playful. Two slim fingertips brush his lower lip. He's watching me like he's remembering too. How I kissed that jawline. Nipped it with my teeth when he withheld his kisses and drove me to the brink of begging.

Silence stretches. My thighs clench.

'We'll need to be convincing,' he says quietly. 'In public. Around my grandfather. That means touching. Eye contact. Chemistry. And less of wishing me to hell. It might convince him if he's feeling particularly onerous. Or it might make him question your true motives.'

My true motives. I force a breath out slowly and try not to squirm in my seat.

'You said that before. Chemistry won't be a problem,' I say before I can stop myself.

His eyes gleam. 'No, it won't.' He leans in, voice dropping to that low rumble that used to echo in my bones. 'We'll need to be comfortable kissing. Holding each other. This farce won't work if we act like we're allergic to each other.'

A churn of confusion knots my stomach. 'You blacklisted me like yesterday's gossip and now you want banter?' I step back, pulse thudding. 'What game are you playing, Ashon?'

He tilts his head, expression unreadable. 'Call it rehearsal. You succeeded in pulling the proverbial wool over my eyes like a pro before. Let's see if your acting skills are still award-worthy.'

Heat floods my neck—part fury, part reluctant ache. 'Don't,' I whisper, though I'm not sure if it's warning or plea.

But he keeps coming. Of course he does. 'You'll have to let me touch you like I did that night. Like I remember. Think you can manage, Miss Rockson?'

I suck in a breath. 'Do you? Remember?' *Dammit.* Why am I rehashing this? Glutton for punishment much?

'Every second,' he breathes. But it's impossible to tell if recollection pleases or infuriates. His smile is slow and lethal. 'Every. Detail. When your hands were in my hair and you whispered my name like it meant something,' he continues, 'So decide now, Cilla—can you stomach pretending you still burn for me, or should I find someone who can lie better?'

God.

My thighs clench and I fight the surge of arousal I haven't felt since—

No.

No.

'I told you not to go there,' I snap, trying to hold onto logic, air, anything that isn't this sudden rush of want.

He lifts his hands in mock surrender, but his voice is all gravel, with heat and deadly, ruthless intent. 'We're supposed to be in love, Cilla. If I can't talk about it, how the hell are we going to convince anyone it's real?'

I press my palm to my chest, grounding myself. 'We don't need to talk about it. We just need to *act.* And you might be used to playing pretend, Ashon, but some of us don't have the luxury of blurring the lines.'

His brow furrows. 'What does that mean?'

I shake my head. 'Nothing. Forget it.'

Focus.

Stay sharp.

He's not here for you. He's here for your performance. You're here for your justice.

And yet… I can still feel the heat of his skin. The memory of his mouth, hot and reverent. The way he whispered, grief-shrouded, *'stay'* that probably wasn't intended for me when I was already halfway out the door.

I drag in a breath. 'So what's next, boss?'

His eyes flick to my mouth. 'Next? We sleep.'

'Separately,' I say quickly.

That damn mocking, belly-flipping half-smile again that triggers all sorts of warning bells I *should* heed. 'For now.'

Ashon

The sun is molten gold as we descend into Kotoka International Airport, but all I feel is the dull pressure of history pressing in.

Ghana is beautiful. Vibrant. Alive in a way Los Angeles could never be. But being back makes my chest tighten, like I'm bracing for a punch that never lands on time only to land twice as hard when I'm not expecting it.

As the jet touches down, I look across at Cilla.

Her face is unreadable, eyes shielded behind oversized sunglasses. She's changed into a turquoise linen sundress perfect for the punishing temperatures with a matching soft silk scarf knotted at her throat. Renée did an exemplary job, far exceeding my expectations. Everything is plucked straight from Rodeo Drive because Nana notices things like labels.

Cilla sits straight-backed like a queen in exile, ready for war.

God help me, she looks *perfect*.

If only it wasn't the better version of the woman who offered sympathy and mind-blowing sex, then left my bed to pursue her nefarious agenda.

An agenda you're still in the dark about...

It grated that my security team had drawn a blank on her true motives, then and now. That I'm left with the bilious conclusion that it was indeed just gold-digging greed that had led Cilla Rockson to my door.

I surge to my feet the moment the plane stops. Then force the unwanted churning in my gut away.

I'm home. It's time to play this role I never wanted but am forced to enact.

Outside, it's chaos in the best way. A crowd has gathered. Local and international media. Placards and cell phones jostling for position. Courtesy of Renée, I already know what the social media headlines are screeching.

Hollywood's Favourite Son Brings Bride Home.

I hadn't expected this much fanfare. But I should have. Nana Biney orchestrates optics like a maestro. Of course he would turn my homecoming into a circus.

We're met by a traditional dance troupe at the terminal exit. The air pulses with the beat of *fontomfrom* drums, dancers leaping and spinning in vibrant Kente, mimicking the ceremonies of the Year of Return.

Cilla's eyes widen. 'Is this for us?'

I nod. 'Welcome to Bineydom. It's only going to get worse from here. Or better, depending on your outlook.'

The motorcade that whisks us away is pure overkill—four black SUVs flanking a glossy Mercedes Maybach with government plates. Waving crowds. Police escorts. Drones overhead.

'Overcompensating much?' she mutters.

I don't respond. My stomach coils tighter the closer we get to the house.

Nana's house.

No—compound is more accurate.

And courtesy of our mode of transport, we arrive far too quickly.

The Biney residence to the west of Accra is less home and more fortress, a sprawl of ivory pillars and shuttered grandeur perched on ancestral land that smells of history and power. The kind of power that doesn't ask for anything—it simply *expects*. Old money hums in the stone beneath my feet. Portraits of ancestors line the hallway like judges, their eyes oil-painted and watchful, condemning me before I've even stepped through the front doors.

I feel thirteen again. An outsider. Unworthy. Caught between two countries, two cultures, never quite enough of either. Ghanaian in name, but not in voice. American in accent, but never in standing.

Nana never let me forget it.

And I can hear the echoes of the impending judgement, even before I'm in his presence.

Making movies is a child's dream.

Don't throw away your legacy for something cheap and shallow.

I went against his better advice. Built everything from the ground up—studio, name, empire. But still, here I am. Crawling back with a woman I barely trust and a performance I don't want to give, just to prove I'm worthy of land already marked by my bloodline.

He wants a show. He wants respectability. Continuity. He wants *legacy* he can point to before he dies.

So here I am. I glance at her as the front doors swing open, the beat of ceremonial drums rising in the distance.

The irony of it is that she looks like she belongs here more than I ever did.

I fix my jacket, square my shoulders, and step forward into the gilded corridor I once swore I'd never walk again.

Here goes nothing.

Let the performance begin.

Cilla

When Ashon pins me with a piercing stare one second before he offers his arm, I take it. Not because I want to, but because I know how imperative the next ten minutes are. I need to perform. To hold myself like I belong even when my knees are shaking beneath the linen hem of a $5,000 dress.

We walk side by side into the lion's den.

Polished teak floors glow in the amber light of the early evening sun. Baobab trees line the inner courtyard like sentries. Somewhere in the distance, the smell of roasting plantains mingles with frangipani on the breeze.

Nana Biney is a towering figure of old-money Ghanaian aristocracy—regal, ruthless and razor-sharp beneath his dignified exterior. With deep-set, hawk-like eyes, ebony skin burnished by age, and a full white beard trimmed with military precision, he looks every inch the retired elder statesman he is.

Draped in rich *ntoma* with one shoulder bare, he commands the very air like a king holding court. From studying everything I could get my hands on about this man and his ruthless claim, I know his words are few, but each one lands with the weight of legacy and silent threat.

Once the butler ushers us into his presence, I perch on the edge of an ornate wooden chair beside a brass tea table, hands dampening with sweat. My stomach is already unsettled, not just from the nerves, but from the faint suspicion of a secret I haven't verified or dared name. Yet.

Across from me, Old Man Biney watches like a hawk in indigo and gold. Two signet rings glint on his fingers. Nothing about him is soft, but then nothing ever was.

Ashon stands behind me, a shadow carved from mahogany, silent but alert. I can feel him there, just out of reach, the tension in him coiled like rope before a storm.

Nana didn't rise when we approach. Power never needs to stand—it waits to be acknowledged.

'Ashon,' he says, with a nod so slight it barely qualifies as a gesture. 'Back from the land of lights and lies.'

Ashon returns the nod, smooth as silk. 'Nana. It's…good to be home.'

A pause and a silky sound of swords leaving scabbards. A flicker of something cold in the old man's eyes.

'Funny how quickly you return when there's an estate on the line. I don't know whether to wish you *Akwaaba* or not.'

Ashon's lips twitch—an almost-smile, practiced and unreadable. 'Or maybe I missed the sound of your charm.'

Nana's chuckle is dry, edged with warning. 'Don't flatter me, boy. You were born with your father's face and your mother's rebellion. Dangerous combination.'

Ashon doesn't flinch. 'You'll find I'm more practical than rebellious these days.'

'I'll be the judge of that.'

He finally turns to me, his gaze sharp enough to slice through the fabric of my dress. Ashon rests a hand briefly on the curve of my shoulder—possessive, a warning disguised as support. I stiffen, just enough for him to feel it. His hand stays for a moment longer. Just enough to deliver the firmer warning.

'This is Cilla Rockson,' Ashon says smoothly. 'My fiancée.'

'You carry yourself well, Cilla Rockson,' Nana says, voice like gravel dragged across a stone floor. 'But breeding, like a pregnancy, always tells eventually, you know.'

I smile, soft but sharp, even as my heart lurches straight to my heels. 'I was raised to speak when spoken to, sir. And to look a lion in the eye when I meet one.'

He chuckles, low and gravelly. 'Ah. A sharp tongue hidden behind pretty manners. I like that. Tell me, who are your people?'

My spine stiffens. My pulse hammers, but I don't blink. 'My father was a schoolteacher. My mother ran a fabric stall. Hardworking, ordinary people.'

Mostly true. Just not the part about the land. The shame. The whispered secrets that wrapped around our family name like vines. Not the part where I swore on my father's grave that I would get it back.

'From where?' he presses.

I sip my tea. Hot and bitter. Buy myself a little bit of time. 'Central Region. A small town not many remember.'

Something flickers in his eyes. Recognition, maybe. Or suspicion. The name Rockson clearly scrapes at something buried deep. But it's also a name found in many regions of Ghana.

'And when will you marry my grandson?' Nana asks, sharp and sudden. 'Or is this just another Hollywood trial period?' His surprisingly nimble fingers snap. 'What do you call it? An experimental pilot?'

The questions land like a slap.

My fingers tighten around the porcelain. I will them not to shake.

Before I can find my voice, Ashon steps forward. His hand settles again on my shoulder. Warm. Heavy. Grounding. And despite myself, I lean into it, the smallest surrender.

'We'll announce the date soon,' he says, gravel-voiced and sure. 'We wanted to settle in first.'

'You've always run, Ashon,' Nana says, slicing him open with a look. 'From family. From responsibility. But now you bring a woman into my house and expect me to believe you're ready? How do I know it's not one of those cheap reality show set ups?'

Ashon stills behind me. I feel the breath catch in his chest. The primal tension rising inside him. And for the first time I wonder how far he would go for this thing he craves so much. And how far he would go for *a woman* he craved just as much.

Enough. You only just got here. Don't get carried away. Now. Ever.

My cup clinks against the saucer as I set it down with practiced grace. I raise my eyes to Nana, letting steel filter through my voice. 'I don't claim to know everything about your grandson's past, sir. But I know what I see when he talks about the future.'

Nana arches a brow. 'And what is that?'

'Conviction,' I say quietly. 'Fire. A man who wants to build something bigger than himself.' I clench my belly, raise my hand and place it on the one on my shoulder. A picture of solidarity that terrifies me a little because it *should* feel much more difficult than this.

There's a pause. Then he tilts his head, more intrigued than before.

'You speak like someone who understands legacy. Do you want children, Miss Rockson?'

My throat tightens. The question shouldn't feel like a dagger, but it does. A hundred thoughts crash inside me. I don't know how to answer. I barely know how to breathe.

My hand drifts—instinctively—towards—

No.

'Yes,' I say softly. 'One day.'

Nana leans forward. The gold in his rings catches the light like claws. 'A family is more than an inheritance. It is continuity. If you carry his child one day, you will understand. Until then, be careful with his name. It carries weight.'

The words sound harmless but they land exactly like what they are—a warning.

I force a smile, breathe through the nausea curling at the edges of my composure.

'She carries it well already,' Ashon says, voice low and proud.

Nana studies us one last time, then nods. A ruler granting permission. 'Very well. You've had a long journey. Eat something. We will speak again tomorrow. Sleep well, Mrs Biney...soon-to-be.'

He rises and I see he's a few inches shorter than his grandson, but no less formidable. The power shifts as he disappears down the colonnade, leaving the scent of sandalwood and challenge in his wake. And I'm not surprised at all when the power settles on his grandson.

I realise I've been holding my breath for half the conversation but it doesn't come any easier when Ashon's gaze so much more reminiscent of his grandfather's, settles on me.

'He doesn't miss a thing,' I murmur.

'No,' Ashon replies. 'He doesn't. But you handled him admirably enough.'

The compliment warms me, but it also stings. Because it means nothing is real—not even this moment of fragile victory.

'Thanks,' I respond a little sharper than I intended.

His own gaze sharpens, his face tightening a touch. 'Everything okay?'

I nod, though I'm not sure it's true. My heart is a riot. My mind a minefield. His presence makes it worse. Or better. I can't tell. 'I'm fine,' I say, chin raised. 'I told you I could play the role,' I whisper.

'Hmm. So you did. You should remember though that in my world, it requires several takes for a landing to stick. This was merely your first take.'

The words hang there between us, thick with tension and something dangerously close to longing. The reminder from him of what we are—strangers, enemies, actors in a farce—burns a little, which is absurd.

I should get up. Walk away. But I don't and neither does he. We sit there, two actors still in costume, the performance clinging to our skin like sweat. The air is heavy with what we didn't say in front of Nana—our sordid one-night history, our mutual distrust, the sharp awareness that even pretend intimacy has a body count. I hate how my body leans towards his heat, even as my mind warns me to keep my distance.

Ashon shifts beside me, that unreadable look back in his eyes, the one that says he sees too much and trusts too little. 'Don't forget your lines, *Mrs Biney*,' he murmurs, voice low, mocking and lethal. Then he rises, leaving behind only his cologne, his tension and the distinct sense that the real performance, the one that could ruin us both, hasn't even begun.

The suite is decadent in a way that makes my breath catch. High ceilings draped in gauze, carved mahogany furniture polished to a mirror sheen, soft golden light glowing from sconces shaped like twisted vines. The kind of space that's meant to seduce, not soothe. Floor-to-ceiling windows open onto a private garden bathed in moonlight, the scent of jasmine thick in the air.

And in the centre of the room, like a loaded weapon, is a single, enormous four-poster bed.

I stop dead in the doorway, growing cold, then hot. Far too hot. 'No,' I mutter. 'Absolutely not.'

Ashon steps past me like he owns the oxygen in the room, already loosening his jacket. 'Problem?'

I shoot him a look that could split concrete. 'One bed? Under your grandfather's roof? Really?'

He doesn't flinch. 'We're almost married, claiming a relationship that includes intimacy. It would be suspicious otherwise.'

'There are entire wings of this house,' I hiss, crossing my arms. 'Multiple suites with connecting rooms. East-facing, discreet, perfect for guests of status. I know for a fact other rooms on this floor connect to others with their own ensuite.'

His brows lift, and I wince inwardly at the unwieldy slip. 'And how would you know that?'

I hesitate only for a breath. 'I read it in some architectural magazine somewhere, I'm sure.'

He doesn't bother to hide the deep scepticism in the smile that curves his lips. 'Always so thorough.' He shrugs off his jacket and tosses it onto the bed, watching me with that maddening glint in his eyes. 'It's the 21st century, sweetheart. People survive shared mattresses. And as you've been at pains to insist, there will be no touching outside my grandfather's presence and especially in private. Or is this something else?' he stares at me with piercing eyes. 'Are you worried about slipping in private, Miss Rockson?'

I roll my eyes to hide my throbbing pulse and the heat pooling between my thighs as my gaze darts between his face and the bed. 'Absolutely not. But the fact remains that your grandfather is the picture of old-school conservative.'

'And he's also a man with a dozen ulterior motives firing off at any one time,' he counters in a tone outwardly casual, but there's an undercurrent of mockery and acerbic amusement. 'Maybe he wants a great-grandchild sooner rather than later.'

My spine stiffens. My hands clench.

I don't answer.

Because even now, even in this absurd palace of privilege and performance, I can't deny the low flutter in my belly.

The possibility that terrifies me. The secret I haven't spoken aloud even to myself.

The possibility that maybe—just maybe—that great-grandchild isn't a pipe dream but a reality already growing inside me.

CHAPTER THREE

Ashon

I CAN'T STOP watching her. And it's maddening in the extreme.

A mere forty-eight hours after our arrival, Cilla glides through the Biney estate like she was born to it, barely faltering. She smiles at the kitchen staff, charms my grandmother's nurse, asks thoughtful questions about the art on the walls and about the gardener's family.

She's *flawless*. Too flawless.

We're attending a state charity gala tonight, at Nana's insistence. Cilla wears a gold silk gown that hugs her curves in all the ways I remember, playing havoc with my insides. It's annoying and disturbing that I haven't been able to take a full breath since she came down the stairs, fully absorbed in her role.

On our arrival, she took my arm and walked into the ballroom like it was the most natural thing in the world.

We dance, pose for photos, do interviews with Ghanaian press. She plays the part so well I almost forget it's all a game.

Almost.

I don't miss that she's found an excuse to head for the ladies room more than twice now, or that when the night fades into the thrum of cicadas and the scent of hibiscus on the breeze, she leaves my side, heading for the relative solitude of the terrace.

If she needs a breather, I should let her have it. She's played her part exemplarily tonight. And yet…

I step out before I can will my body to behave otherwise, to not *hunger* for this…for her. There are few million women in the world who will welcome my attention, *after* this little production is done and I've achieved my—

God, the way the moonlight touches her skin like a lover.

Just like that night...in my bed.

My body remembers hers, instinctively. The scent of her. The soft sound she made when I kissed her throat.

She turns, sees me and her breath catches.

'Ashon…what do you…' She glances behind me. 'Am I needed back in?' she asks, a trace of something sharp in her voice.

I wave that away. 'We've done enough for tonight, I think,' I murmur.

She turns fully, arms folded across her middle, but it's not in coldness—more like protection. Against me. Against the memory that simmers between us, potent and poisonous. The urge to question her, dig deeper into her own motives, strikes again but I push it away. *I don't care.*

To preserve the status quo or because you don't want to be disappointed?

Neither. *Both.*

I grit my teeth against the mocking voice and cross the terrace slowly, unwilling to break the spell of her standing there under the stars, wrapped in a sunset-hued Kente shawl that makes her skin glow like caramel dipped in gold. Her braids are pinned into a soft knot. Her neck bared like an invitation I know better than to accept. Still, I offer her the champagne flute in my hand.

'For celebration of a job well done tonight,' I say. 'Or maybe to just…survival.'

She doesn't take it.

'No thanks,' she replies, her voice measured. 'I'd rather not add booze to the mix. After all, alcohol was part of the mess before, wasn't it?'

I blink, jaw clenched at the memory I don't need. The bottle. The numbness I chased. The taste of guilt the morning after.

Her refusal lands like a punch, more telling than she realises. But she's careful—too careful.

I'll remind you why you should've stayed in your side of town.

I should probe that threat too, dismantle that landmine before it blows up in my face, especially if it's connected to whatever games she's got going on beneath that breathtaking surface.

Instead, I lift my own glass and toast the distance between us.

'To fakery, then.'

Her gaze holds mine, unwavering. 'And to remembering that it's only ever that.'

But as she brushes past me to head back inside, her shoulder grazes mine and the jolt is real. Instant. Intimate. *Dangerous.*

I stay rooted on the terrace, alone with my drink and the echo of her warmth, wondering why that bite of hers sparks a thrill of…something inside me.

And why the idea of playing with Cilla Rockson's fire—a surprisingly salacious thought—along with using her the way she intended to use me, makes me feel more alive than I've ever felt in a long time.

Cilla

The music pulses beneath the hum of laughter and clinking glassware, the air thick with billion-dollar-deals being cut and perfume that costs more than my rent used to.

The evening can't finish quickly enough but I try to smile, to focus on the sweetness of the chocolate mango dessert I foolishly accepted because saying no to everything was drawing eyes my way. But the combination of the sickly taste of the dessert melting on my tongue, and the hyperawareness of the curve of Ashon's palm at my back exacerbates the wave of nausea rolling through me, sharp and relentless.

I excuse myself with a smile I barely hold together and slip away, again, knowing I've done it a few times now, drawn his complete focus I feel at my nape as I dash into the marble-lined washroom for the third time tonight. The second the door clicks shut, I grip the edge of the sink like it might steady me. Until my knuckles ache and my breath stutters in my chest.

In the mirror, I see someone I barely recognise—flawless in silk, with gleaming skin and lips stained hibiscus red. Poised. Beautiful. A woman who looks like she belongs here.

But underneath, I'm…a dozen bags of nerves. What was it Nana Biney said on our first meeting? Character was like pregnancy…it reveals itself eventually?

Unfortunately, so does *actual* pregnancy.

I press a hand to my stomach. Finally acknowledging what I've been hiding from. It's still flat. But I know I can't keep ignoring what could be happening.

What the truth might—

Two women entering drag me from the direction of thoughts I'll have no choice but to parse through, sooner rather than later.

When I step back into the party, I fix my face into something camera-ready. Polished. Distant. But Ashon catches the shift in a heartbeat. His eyes sharpen, trailing me through the crowd like a laser.

'Something disagreeing with you?' he murmurs, eyes far too watchful.

'Just hot,' I lie. 'Still acclimatising I think.'

He doesn't push. But I feel the pressure of his gaze on me, steady and unsettling, through every toast and every saccharine conversation.

I'm so hung up on not giving anything away, I don't see the woman approaching until she's right next to us.

Delphine Daniels.

The stunning woman Ashon dated publicly a few years ago. The woman who shared her heartbreak on social media with the zeal of an Oscar-hungry actress and ostensibly sold every intimate detail of their time together to every tabloid in existence.

The woman I suspect is responsible for Ashon throwing that chilling 'gold digger' label at me.

She slinks over in crimson silk, all teeth and legs and malice disguised as charm. 'I see you've finally decided to settle down, Ashon. I was beginning to think Hollywood made you forget your roots.'

'I never forget my roots,' he says coolly but subtle tension rides his broad shoulders.

Her eyes slice to me. 'And your fiancée? Is she enjoying Ghana? Or just the spotlight?'

I smile. Sweet. Lethal. 'I don't need the spotlight, Miss Daniels. But thank you for the warm welcome.'

Ashon's fingers find mine, his grip possessive. But maybe in warning too. I let him. For now. Just long enough for Delphine's eyes to narrow and her smile to fall flat before she rallies, and the killer smile resurfaces, slippery and hungry.

'Well, if the *spotlight* ever proves too much for her, I'd be more than happy to…ease the pressure. I learned a thing or two the last time.' Her hungry gaze lingers on Ashon. 'Let's catch up. For old times' sake.'

She trails a manicured finger down Ashon's lapel like she has the right.

I force myself not to stiffen. Or flinch. I just tilt my head, letting my smile stretch wider. 'He doesn't do reruns, Miss Daniels. But I'm sure you can pitch yourself to Netflix.'

Her mouth twitches, her eyes darkening with malice. But before she can recover, the nausea comes back—hard. Like someone lit a fuse in my gut. The room tilts.

Ashon turns to me instantly. His free arm slides around my waist with jarring tenderness but a quick glance up shows a frown forming on his face, questions brimming in his eyes.

Questions I'm in no mood to answer. Maybe he sees that, which is why his lips thin.

'We're leaving,' he grates, his voice like iron wrapped in silk.

Delphine blinks. 'Already? But the night's just—'

'Over.' His tone brooks no argument.

He doesn't wait for her response. Just steers me away, palm warm against my spine. Heads swing our way, including Nana's and his grandmother's but Ashon doesn't stop, nor even acknowledge them. And I hate to admit it, but it's a powerful, heady feeling to be in the wake of a man like him doing exactly what he wants.

Only when it suits you though, right?

I suppress a bite of shame because it's true. Wanting to leave and being granted exactly that is welcome in the moment, but I can't forget that the Bineys taking exactly what they wanted shattered my family's dreams.

But it's not just the heat.

Ashon leans in, voice low, brushing the edge of my bare shoulder. ‘What’s wrong?’

‘Nothing.’ The word slips out too quickly, too easily.

‘You were glowing half an hour ago. Now you look like you’ve been through a war.’

‘I told you. I’m fine.’ My voice is clipped, and I hate how brittle it sounds.

Outside the crowd parts like water in front of us and minute later, we’re in the car.

Silence stretches taut between us.

‘You looked like you were about to faint back there,’ Ashon drops silkily into the dark interior.

I stare straight ahead, ignoring the piercing stare. ‘I didn’t.’

‘You barely ate anything all evening too.’ He leans back, jaw tight. ‘Was it Delphine?’

I blink. Then narrow my eyes. ‘You tell me,’ I say, ice in my tone. ‘Is she part of this elaborate performance too? Or was that her trying to stake a claim?’

His brows rise. ‘She’s part of my past. One you rightly pointed out I don’t intend to revisit.’

‘She didn’t seem to think that,’ I snap.

He peers at me, an enigmatic look in his eyes. ‘That’s her problem not mine. And is that jealousy I hear?’

Hot and cold waters of chagrin rush through me. ‘Don’t flatter yourself.’

His nostrils flares. ‘She’s nothing to me. Hasn’t been in years. She showed me her true colours and I took note.’

‘And yet you didn’t exactly shut her down.’

He shoots me a look. ‘You really want me to start publicly defending my *fake fiancée* from my ex-girlfriend? That’s the circus you want?’

I press my lips together. The silence stretches.

Then his voice hardens. ‘Delphine doesn’t matter. But you

however… I'm not sure whether to applaud how you're playing this part or be intensely wary with the way you're messing with my focus in a way that seems…far too effective for our purposes.'

My heart skips, just once. Then races. God help me—I think I like it that way.

I snap. 'I'm not even going to bother asking if that's a compliment or an insult. Look, I'm just doing my job. Smiling, charming Nana, pretending this circus isn't slowly driving me insane while your ex tries to eye-fuck you across the room. Just let me be.'

He doesn't answer but the silence weighs heavier and my insides clench, wondering if like the champagne from before, I'm risking exposure.

'What are you not telling me?' His voice is rougher now. Sharper. *Deadlier.*

I close my eyes, then rush to open them again when the image of myself in the ladies room mirror invades my brain.

I might be pregnant. I don't know what I'm doing. I'm scared out of my mind because it'll change everything. Or nothing.

Thankfully, the words stick in my throat. 'Not everything is about you, Ashon.'

One brow arches and I feel the full power of his regard. 'Is it not? Because I was of the opinion that that was exactly what the next few months of our lives are about.'

I grit my teeth, let the silence spell out my displeasure. Luckily, he takes the hint or, more likely, doesn't feel the need to respond because he's said his piece.

When we arrive, I don't wait for him. My heels echo down the marble corridor as I head towards the east wing. But instead of going to my bedroom, I slip into the guest bathroom and shut the door behind me, fighting another bout of nausea and the mocking voice now screeching in my head.

One missed period, I could blame on stress. Losing my job. Getting blacklisted by a man who's now pretending to be my fiancé.

But two?

Two periods late, and not a single cramp. No sore breasts, no moods swings fully-funded by PMS. And I *almost* slipped up on the terrace, turning down the champagne too fast, too pointedly.

I sink onto the bench and drop my head into my hands. I can't pretend any more. I can't keep brushing it off like I have time.

My hand drifts to my belly before I realise what I'm doing. I catch myself just in time.

But the thought takes deeper root, as does the possibility that my entire life might be about to implode.

The Accra sun is merciless.

It presses down from a cloudless sky, a molten weight that turns the red Ghanaian earth into a clay furnace. The scent of dust, shea butter, diesel fumes, and roasting peanuts from roadside vendors hangs heavy in the air, clinging to my skin like a film of anxiety. My dress—a sleek, designer take on an Ankara silhouette with a cinched waist and exaggerated sleeves—is stunning, camera-ready. And sticking to my back in all the worst places.

We're here for a Biney Foundation outreach day—some long-standing charity Nana supports that partners with local NGOs to offer maternal health checkups, micro-loans for market women, and food programs for underfed schoolchildren. The whole thing has been carefully curated for maximum press coverage and minimum sincerity. Still, some of the volunteers are kind. Most of the women shake my hand and stare like I'm something foreign, distant, unreal. I want to scream that I'm one of them, but I don't.

A child presses a wilted hibiscus flower into my palm. I crouch and murmur something gentle—about how pretty it is, how grateful I am—but the words scrape like gravel. My heels sink into the dirt and my smile stays plastered on like a shield.

All morning I've been thinking about the box hidden under the sink in our shared suite. Two slim white sticks. One pink-wrapped test. I bought it early, before sunrise, at a pharmacy far from the estate under the pretext of going for a walk. I've yet to take it.

I don't know what I want it to say.

Positive means everything changes. Every lie gets heavier. It means facing the one truth I've buried the deepest—that part of me doesn't absolutely recoil in horror of piling one night of misjudgement with a life-long consequence. That part of me wonders what it would be like to carry a child—Ashon Biney's child.

And then there's my mother, who still hasn't forgiven me for that hasty phone call I made to her three nights ago, after accepting Ashon's deal. For the not-fully-thought-through-in-hindsight plan of inveigling my way into a housekeeping position and getting close to a Biney in the first place.

How on earth would I explain this?

I force another smile as the camera shutters click and a journalist barks questions I don't bother registering.

Ashon is beside me, cool as ever in an ivory linen suit, holding court with donors and grinning for the press. He looks composed, aristocratic, annoyingly unruffled. Like he was born to wear this life. And maybe he was.

I want to resent him for dragging me into this charade. For

being the reason I'm suffocating in fakery, ignoring my body and another bout of rising nausea, and smiling when I want to scream. But mostly, I want to sit. Or cry. Or run.

The nausea hits suddenly, sharp and merciless.

I grip the edge of a vendor's table, swaying slightly as an older woman explains something about the logistics of food deliveries. I nod blindly, her voice slipping over me like heat haze.

Ashon turns towards me, sensing the shift.

'Cilla?' he asks, deep voice low but alert.

I open my mouth to respond, but no words come. The sun pulses behind my eyes. My heart thunders in my ears. The air thickens, and I can't seem to draw breath.

Then a wave of vertigo slams into me.

The drums distort. Faces blur. Ashon's voice stretches, urgent and far away.

'Cilla!'

And then—everything goes black.

I wake to the hiss of air-conditioning and the dull throb of pain blooming behind my eyes. The white ceiling above me is blinding. There's a faint antiseptic sting in the air, and the soft click of machines nearby. An IV drips into my arm, cool and slow.

My mouth is dry, my skin clammy.

I don't even need to open my eyes to know I'm not alone. That my formidable fake fiancé is very much present. No doubt tracking my every breath because my very skin feels the force of his undivided attention.

And he's pacing.

Back and forth across the room like a caged lion in one of those gilded zoos rich people pretend is natural. Except there's nothing natural about the charged emotion radiating off him in waves.

He stops the second I move. I pry my eyes open.

'Cilla.' My name is a clipped acknowledgement as he closes the distance to my side in three long strides.

He's shed his jacket and his sleeves are rolled up on brawny arms. It truly is unspeakably unfair how hot he looks, even playing the role of worried fiancé.

'What happened?' I ask, even though I knew this was coming. That my head-in-the-sand moments were numbered.

'You fainted. At the charity event. You scared the hell out of everyone.'

Including you? I want to ask, but I don't. 'I—' My throat sticks. 'I don't remember.'

'You dropped like a stone in front of three cameras. Do you have any idea how that looked?'

It sounds very much like an admonition but there's something almost…shaken behind the words. And that watchfulness is back. The one I feel I could never hide from even at the farthest corner of the galaxy.

'I didn't do it for the publicity,' I rasp. 'It was the heat.'

His eyes narrow. 'The heat is oppressive, I'll accept that but was it just the heat?'

I lick my bottom lip to buy time I might not be able to afford. 'What's that supposed to mean?'

His gaze scours me from head to toe and back again. 'You've lost weight and call it wild instincts blurring but you're withholding something. I think it's in your best interest to tell me now rather than later,' he says with chilling insistence.

Before I can summon heat and outrage or scramble for a pithy response to hide the dread crawling through me, the door swings open and a doctor in a crisp white coat breezes in, flipping through a chart with the practiced ease of someone used to delivering all kinds of news.

'Ah, Miss Rockson. Good to see you're awake. I'm happy to report there's nothing untoward to worry about. Your vitals are stable,' she says brightly, giving me a quick once-over. 'Your blood sugar dipped—likely due to the heat, dehydration and…' Her gaze flicks down to the chart again. 'Pregnancy.'

The word hangs in the air like a flare.

She looks up with a too-cheerful smile. 'You'll need plenty of rest. Light meals, fluids every hour and absolutely no prolonged exposure to this Accra sun. And no stress if you can help it.' Her eyes twinkle, as if that last part is a joke only I can't laugh at. 'Congratulations, by the way.'

I blink. 'Sorry—umm, what?' I stammer, but she's already gone.

The door clicks softly shut behind her. The room seems to still. Stretch. Tighten.

My throat closes. My hand instinctively presses to my abdomen.

Ashon doesn't speak. And he probably doesn't need to. With the air between us suddenly electrified and heavy, every second seems to shriek loud and condemning.

When I chance a glance at the man frozen at the foot of my bed, he's statue-still, but his eyes…*awurade*…his eyes are grappling hooks, fastening me in place.

I swallow. 'Ashon—'

His gaze sharpens even more lethally. 'You're pregnant?'

I don't answer because I can't. Saying I didn't know feels… sounds disingenuous. But I don't even need to. My silence says enough but whether it spells my damnation I'm about to find out.

'Answer me, Cilla.' His voice rises, jagged and sharp. 'You're pregnant?'

'Sounds like it.' And there it is. Simple. Unavoidable. And yet it tastes like glass.

He stills. Like a storm eye before it visits devastation on everything in its path. *Me.*

And then he laughs, low and humourless. 'Of course. Of course you are.'

'Ashon—'

His hand slashes through the air, silencing me. 'This is why you agreed so fast. The conditions. The fake relationship. The promises. The mysterious ask reserved for later. You were already playing your next move. Your ultimate ace in the hole.'

I sit up, heart hammering, the IV tugging slightly at my arm. 'How dare you. That's not at all what I—'

'What you planned?' he spits. 'Get pregnant? Let me catch feelings? Reel in the Biney fortune? God, Cilla, I was right, wasn't I? I played right into your hands.' There's ashen mockery in there with a shocked, heavy dose of it aimed at himself. As if the Great Ashon Biney can't believe he's been swindled.

I straighten my spine, even as my insides churn. 'I didn't plan this. And I didn't tell you because I… I thought it was still…unlikely. Because I needed space to figure things out for myself if—' My words freeze as he stiffens even harder. 'I guess I mostly didn't tell you because I knew you'd react exactly like this.'

His eyes blaze. 'So what? I'm just supposed to accept it? Take your word that I'm the father and carry on like everything's fine? Do you know how cliché this play is?'

My hands tighten in the hospital sheet. 'In your world, maybe. In mine, you're supposed to trust me. But clearly, that hasn't even occurred to you.'

'Nice try, attempting to flip this onto me.'

'I'm not attempting anything. I suspected. I never got

around to verifying. That's the truth whether you accept it or not.'

His nostrils flare and even before he opens his mouth, I know I'll despise what comes out of it. 'I'll accept it. After you take a DNA test.'

I freeze. 'Absolutely not.'

His nostrils flare. 'Why the hell not? We're in the right place for it. I see no reason to delay or refuse. Unless there's something you want to admit?'

I glare every ounce of hatred I possess for the implication and for this man and everything he stands for. 'Something like what, exactly?' He opens his mouth and I slam up my hand before he can speak. 'Actually, stop. Because if you're about to say what I think you are, I can't account for what I'll do.'

Ashon displays not a single ounce of remorse or regret for the unstated slur. 'This is resolved very simply. Prove it.'

'No, I will not. Because I'm not going to let you put me on trial for something I didn't do.' My voice is sharp now, my temper finally clawing its way out. 'I'm not some con artist trying to score a Biney heir. You don't get to accuse me of trapping you and then demand my blood.'

'You think I'm just going to roll over and accept this? You drop this on me like a grenade—'

'It's not a grenade. It's a baby.' I breathe, voice shaking but steady. 'And whether you like it or not, that baby's already growing inside me. I didn't ask for this. I didn't scheme for it. But I'm dealing with it.'

He's silent. For once.

I rise to my feet, wobbling only slightly. My whole body feels too light and too heavy all at once. Like my emotions have outgrown me. He frowns and starts to reach for me. 'You need to stay in bed—'

I snatch myself out of his reach. 'You want to control this

the way you control everything else in your life?' I whisper. 'Then here's the harsh truth. This time things are out of your control. We did this together so you don't get to dictate things out of guilt or anger or pride. And you sure as hell don't get to punish me for not living up to the fantasy you constructed for your own benefit.'

I brush past him, pulse pounding, leaving behind the antiseptic walls, the IV, the bombshell I left behind and the man who made me feel seen for a single night—before making me feel disposable.

And outside the door, I pause. Press my palm against my belly.

And breathe.

I might have scored a point just now, but I have very little doubt that Ashon Biney will recoup his shock, strategize and come at me even stronger.

And I'll need to be prepared.

CHAPTER FOUR

Ashon

By evening, the house is humming with quiet chaos.

Whispers leak through the corridors like smoke. The staff have that overly polite stiffness and hidden smiles and sparkling smiles that signal they know too much. That the gossip mills are stuffed to overbursting.

I barely hear them. My ears are still ringing with Cilla's words from hours ago.

Pregnant.

Cilla is pregnant. And not just with any child.

Mine.

The second she swept out of the hospital room, head held high in regal hauteur and unbridled acrimony, my knees gave way. I allowed myself a moment of absolute dumbfounded shock. Well. Several moments.

A sliver of guilt at the outrage and…hurt… I spotted in her eyes.

Then I rallied because I was a Biney. Because I had no choice.

And because…a bizarre kind of *elation* had built inside me then, perched on the side of the bed she'd just vacated in the hospital room. One that mocked me for that strenuous demand for a DNA test when I didn't really want one.

Not because as per my instruction a few days ago, my security had come through with the preliminary report on Cilla that detailed her activities mostly since she left my bed that morning. A report that showed no presence of a boyfriend or lover before or after me. But because I already felt a primal possessiveness over the child growing in her womb. A kind I'd experienced for very little in my life, probably save the project close to my heart.

And if for a split second, God help me, I imagined that child with her eyes and my name, entertained the thought of a family I hadn't planned for but didn't entirely hate the thought of, I buried it quickly. Buried that dangerous, premature flicker of possibilities.

I had no business wanting a future with a woman I couldn't trust. A woman whose secrets still made my skin itch. So I filed the feeling away, like I always did.

But I'm not ashamed to admit to myself and no one else, that the sensation had...*alarmed* with its rate of growth over the next few hours. With the fervent need to if not replicate, then at least aspire to the kind of relationship I had with my late father and that I do not have with my grandfather. A relationship that had been the one guiding light in my life. One whose loss I feel deeply and keenly even now.

One that—were I inclined to believe the pronouncements of the elders—was being given a chance at reincarnation by the ancestors?

All of that had been enough for me to expend a lot of energy for the entire afternoon in trying to keep my mind—and my grandfather—from imploding.

He'd summoned us the moment the news trickled up through the household, faster than I could control. Probably from one of the drivers or one of the distant cousins with too much time and too little tact. Or even from the staff at the hospital, eager for a boon from the great man himself.

Now, we stand before Nana Biney in his private study, the place where all decrees are made, often without argument. Cilla is still wearing that haughty expression that says, 'come at me at your peril'. And dear heaven, but why does that spark all sorts of sensations inside me?

Just to test that fire, and apparently because I'm in the mood to toy with my self-preservation, I wrap my hand around her waist, pull her closer to my body. A body I feel a distinct and entirely inappropriate sense of ownership towards now I know it's carrying my seed.

Surprisingly, disarmingly and, yes, also interestingly, she doesn't pull away. Which means she's not inclined to pull the trigger on our little deal.

Because she's holding back for when it counts most?

Cynicism rises and I only know it has resulted in a firmer hold when she shoots me a warning glance.

I exhale, relax my hold but don't let her go, because I'm not inclined to.

Gold filigree frames the windows. Ornate swords hang along the walls, a reminder of the bloodline I belong to. That I can't escape.

He's seated in his favourite armchair, eyes heavy with judgement.

'A child,' he says slowly, each word a stone dropping into still water. 'Out of wedlock. Under this roof?'

I stiffen. 'It wasn't planned. And with respect, *paapa*, I'm a grown man who no longer lives under your roof.'

Cilla doesn't say anything, but perhaps it's my imagination that I sense her surprise and her approval. Her hands are clasped tightly in front of her, head aloft and her gaze now pinned to the bookshelf over Nana's shoulder.

Nana's gaze sharpens like a blade. 'Be that as it may, I'm still the head of this family and some things will be done *my* way. Forget this months-long engagement business. You'll marry immediately. Before this scandal undoes everything I've built.'

I don't flinch. I've been expecting it.

Still, the words fall from my mouth, cool and controlled, even as something twists hard inside my chest. Something that tells me a reckoning is coming. 'Fine. We'll marry immediately.'

Cilla jerks her head towards me, stunned. 'That's it? Just like that?'

I meet her gaze. Her expression is blistering—disbelief and censure flickering in her dark eyes. She looks like a woman who could set fire to everything I've built with nothing but her silence. And God help me, I still want her.

I force a steady breath. '*Paapa* is right. We were going to do this anyway,' I say, directing the next words towards my grandfather, who watches us like a hawk tracking a fault line. 'But this is about doing right by the woman I chose, not saving face or curtailing family scandals. If this is going to be my future, it won't be delayed or negotiated like a contract.'

Nana leans back in his chair, golden rings catching the light. He strokes his jaw once, contemplative. 'So you've made your decision, Ashon.'

'I have.'

'Good.' He turns to Cilla. 'And you, girl? If this is real, if you mean to tie yourself to my grandson, surely you have no objections to doing it swiftly.'

The room feels suddenly airless. My pulse hammers in my ears.

Cilla's jaw tenses. I feel the fury radiating off her, the helplessness she's trying not to show.

She doesn't answer right away.

So I step closer, the weight of performance and something unspoken tightening in my throat. 'You told me you were in this. All in,' I murmur. 'I believed you. Let's stop pretending you don't want to be mine as quickly as I want to be yours,' I drawl, infusing possessive sentiment into my voice that feels not at all performative. That feels—in this new reality of claiming what's mine—astonishingly imperative.

She blinks. Her hand curls into a fist at her side. And I know she hears the trap in my voice, the ruthless hunger that wasn't supposed to be there.

But in this house, beneath Nana's scrutiny, choices vanish fast. And we're running out of air.

Let her walk away and it'll all unravel. Let her stay and we both step into the unknown, but little does she know, the unknown, the daring, is where I thrive. Where the man whose presence I miss and whose memory I intend to carry through my child, taught me to claim. To own.

So I stare her down, curbing the need to bare my teeth, to show her the lion beneath the designer suit.

Your move, Rockson.

Cilla lifts her chin, eyes glittering now. 'Can I speak to Ashon alone?'

Nana's eyes narrow at her audacity, but after a beat, he rises and glides out with the weight of royalty and age. The door closes with a soft click.

I brace myself.

Cilla turns on me, arms folded. 'You arrogant bastard.'

I arch a brow. 'You claim the child you're carrying is mine. Given that I'm choosing to believe you, you didn't think I'd want to make it right?'

'Make it right?' she echoes, laughing bitterly. 'You mean

lay claim. Wrap it all up in your tidy, powerful package. Control it.'

I step closer. 'You think I'll stand by and let my child be born without my name? Without my protection?'

'You think this child is some pawn in your inheritance game?' Her voice cuts, sharp and breathless.

I pause. Because beneath all her fury, I can see it. The hurt and the fear. The resilience holding her together like gold seams in cracked porcelain. Then I shrug. 'You've presented me with a real cherry on top of a fake cake we baked together. I'm doing what needs to be done.'

'I'll marry you, Ashon,' she says, calm and clear. 'But on my terms.'

My body goes taut and I thoroughly despise the feeling that too much resembles bracing myself for an unfathomable impact. Perhaps even a seismic one. I narrow my eyes. 'I'm listening.'

'One. Separate rooms. Make up whatever story you want to, I don't care. I'm not here to warm your bed.'

'You weren't supposed to last time, either.'

She ignores me but her nostrils flare in outrage. 'Two. After the wedding, we drop the charade. No more touching me whenever you feel like it. And you do whatever is needed to ensure your grandfather gives you what you want.'

'What's the hurry?'

She casts a look, defiant with a touch of desperation. 'Because I don't want to be here longer than I need to be. I want to return to the States. And I assume you want to as well.'

There's a beat. Something twists in my chest. Old and stubborn. But I kill it before it can bloom. My mouth curls, brutal and self-protective. 'Darling, that was always the agreement.'

But we both know that's not true.

Because once again the chemistry that had crept in and

drowned us was circling in. Quiet and dangerous. Reminding us that it'd pulled at us and we'd both revelled in it.

And now something else is growing between us.

More dangerous than secrets.

More permanent than spite or lust.

She's carrying my child.

And even though I've convinced myself this marriage is a solution, not a sentiment…the impending reckoning presses harder. 'Anything else on this interesting list of yours?'

Then she says the last one, slow and deliberate, after the briefest of hesitations.

'Did you ever bother to look into the origins of this so-called legacy you're determined to claim?'

Something sharp and hot lances me. 'What are you talking about?'

Her lips firm and she shakes her head with something close to pity. 'You were right. That night in your study, I saw the blueprints for your precious studio. And the land it's being built on. Land that far exceeds what your studio needs.'

'So?'

A fire burns in her eyes, fierce and pure. 'So did you know my family owned a quarter of it? Before your grandfather swooped in and claimed it for expansion?'

The words land like a slap. My pulse stutters. 'So you were creeping around for evidence to do what, exactly? To pull some sort of revenge heist? Humiliate the Bineys in the press? Dismantle my inheritance one damning press story at a time?'

My voice is low, sharp-edged with disbelief, but underneath it, something brittle splinters. Because perhaps I'd held onto some misguided notion that I'd guarded myself against history repeating itself. That I was infallible to such antics.

Bitterness curls through me as I watch her, a part of me abstractedly impressed when she doesn't even flinch.

When the fire in her eyes grows, holier, purer. As if she's the wronged one in this.

She lifts her chin, voice steady but trembling at the edges. 'You think this is about headlines? I was chasing justice… reparations for a family stripped of their future so yours could hoard power dressed up as legacy.' Her fingers curl into fists, small but mighty. 'If greed built your empire, I had every right to go looking for what was stolen.'

I open my mouth, no doubt to deliver something scathing but she beats me to it. 'It was a cocoa farm. Small, but thriving. My mother's pride. My grandfather's and father's livelihood. My childhood.' Her voice is steady, but I can hear the cracks beneath it. 'When the Biney name started stretching into the Western Region, your grandfather offered to buy the land. My family refused. So he used pressure. Influence. Quiet threats. And eventually he got it.' She delivers a scathing laugh filled with judgement. 'On paper it was clean. But only because the family was bleeding by then. Drowning in debt.'

I try to swallow but my throat's dry. 'And why didn't anyone fight it?'

She laughs softly. Bitter. 'Are you serious? You don't think we tried? But what does a common farmer have against the might of Nana Biney? And you know the worst of it? He let the land rot. Left it fallow like it meant nothing. While my father drank his shame and my mother got sick trying to keep us afloat. If not for my uncle who helped me secure a scholarship and gave my mother a roof of her head, I don't know—' She stops for a moment, but I don't need a clearer picture drawn.

A silence stretches between us like a wound.

Then she goes on, full of rancour and jagged pride. 'To your grandfather, it…we were a footnote. One line on his endless balance sheet to be passed onto…you, it seems. A piece of leverage. But to us, it was the difference between survival and ruin.'

And shit, I remember…because haven't I spend far too much time perusing every scrap of paper I can find on what is mine? A forgotten corner of a document years ago. An inherited parcel no one bothered to inspect too closely. A cocoa farm turned red earth. Now prime real estate. The coincidence is too wild to dismiss.

And yet, resist I do. Because the alternative is…is… 'You think this changes things?' I ask coldly. 'You think this little revelation shifts the power dynamic?'

'You think you can sign my life away in marriage and I'd blithely agree without ensuring I fight harder for something for my family and the child I'm carrying? Something that already belongs to me?'

Cold blades slice into my ribs. 'You'd leverage our child?'

She laughs again. 'You dare to condemn me with that tone when you literally did the same? You're leveraging our child to ensure your grandfather plays ball and hands over your precious studio land! And you did it without so much as a by your leave to me. I told you in LA to be careful that you don't make me a pawn. That we're partners. You want marriage? Well, this is me levelling the field you Bineys seem to think belongs only to you,' she says, her beautiful eyes defiant.

My chest burns. Fury and disbelief war with something deeper, darker, more dangerous.

'You've had this up your sleeve all this time,' I say, low and lethal, 'and yet you expect me to believe our every interaction wasn't premeditated? That you didn't step into that housekeeper job with your eyes on my name, my wealth, my land?'

Her eyes flash. 'Keep your name and your wealth. I'll sign

whatever paper you want to that effect if you want. But yes, I want what's mine. What's always been mine.'

My laugh is hollow. Bitter. I didn't think she was different… Dammit. Letting my guard down once was bad enough, but twice? 'And what? Now you think you have me between a rock and a hard place?' I step closer, letting the full weight of my glare meet hers. 'Think again, sweetheart. Winning is in my blood. Forget that at your peril.'

Cilla

The wedding is a spectacle.

A far cry from the quiet registry office ceremony I'd imagined or hoped for.

Nana Biney insists on tradition and optics and spectacle. A royal wedding for a Hollywood heir. An heir with a bride born of muted scandal and servitude.

I am draped in handwoven Kente, dyed in hues of gold and royal purple—colors once reserved for queens. My *gele* is tied into a towering crown by an expert brought in from the top Accra designer house, and my skin gleams under layers of shea butter and gold dust. I am regal. Immaculate. Every inch a Biney bride. And yet, beneath it all, I feel like a puppet in someone else's theatre.

The palace gates of the Biney ancestral home are thrown open.

Thousands gather in the courtyard. Some press against barricades. Others wave miniature Ghana flags and fans to battle the oppressive heat.

Drones hum overhead, capturing every radiant angle of me and Ashon—the prince of Hollywood and his mysterious bride.

'*Dondoo! Ahuonfe* Cilla!' they chant. Beautiful Cilla.

If only.

My name on their lips feels foreign. Unreal.

I'm battling more than nausea. I'm battling deep apprehension and sensation of a silken trap slowly closing in on me.

It's been two long weeks since that bitter exchange the night I agreed to marry him. Since Ashon questioned my motivation and integrity, straining the already thin thread between us.

Two weeks of clipped conversations behind closed doors and choreographed affection in front of Nana. Of strained smiles and calculated touches, rehearsed chemistry for the sake of a legacy we're both wrestling for.

My mother has stopped asking questions. At first, she cried quietly into the phone, disbelief turning to resignation as I explained why I had to do this. How this marriage, this performance, wasn't about revenge any more. It was about reclaiming what was stolen. About giving our name back its dignity.

Now, she understands. Or tries to.

She doesn't know about the baby. Not yet. I'm not ready for that conversation.

But I know.

And knowing has changed me.

I feel it already—this tiny life growing inside me. Unplanned but utterly, irrevocably mine. I talk to it in my head and out loud when no one is listening. I rest my hand on my belly when I sleep. I've stopped hoping it's not real. Because it is.

I love this baby.

I will protect this baby.

And if I have to walk through fire, marry a man I don't trust, and stand alone in a palace full of vultures to secure its future, I will.

Ashon stands beside me, devastating in his *agbada*, black silk trimmed with gold. A lion embroidered across his chest like the family crest. He is every inch the heir.

His hand slips into mine as we step under the ancestral arch. As expensive liquor wets the ground in honour of the ancestors and pleas for a long happy marriage in this life and the next.

His fingers are warm. Steady and searingly familiar. But there's steel in his grip and distance in his eyes. And I quietly admit to myself that he's learned a thing or two from producing and directing. He's learned to play his part, perhaps a little too well.

Because as we say the words and the vows and we're blessed by chiefs and elders, by clergy and ancestors, it all feels too real.

When rice rains like confetti and the drums roll and the gold-tasselled umbrellas follow us everywhere, it's harder not to dip into that make-believe. To wonder what it would be like were this truly the wedding I'd dreamed of as a girl, marrying the man of my dreams.

But thankfully, the moment…*moments* pass.

By the time we arrive at the reception pavilion, I am smiling so hard my cheeks hurt.

I spot my mother first. Her face is pinched into something between pride and concern. My uncle beside her, regal in his own right, eyes unreadable, replacing the dear father who drank himself to death courtesy of the careless suffering the Bineys inflicted on us.

They do not like being the centre of attention and I quietly admit to myself that no, this isn't the kind of justice we imagined. I've dragged them into the limelight with me and regret trawls through me.

We greet guests. Dignitaries. Old women with mischievous eyes and thinly veiled curiosity.

'Ei, soooo beautiful. May the baby be strong like his father.'

'So when is that happening, madam? Don't wait too long, will you?'

My belly clenches. Ashon's hand tightens on my lower back, his thumb brushing low. Almost too low.

Heat floods my cheeks. He leans in, murmuring for my ears only. 'You're going to have to get used to that.'

I glare at him. 'You're enjoying this too much.'

'Am I? My acting skills must be on par with yours then,' he says smoothly, the smile on his lips not reaching his eyes.

We move from table to table, from toast to toast. Laughter. Speeches. Flashing lights. His hand never quite leaves me. Always hovering. *Possessing.*

When it's time for the ceremonial kiss, the guests begin to chant.

'Kiss! Kiss! Kiss!'

Ashon turns to me. His eyes, all fire and ice with heat and mockery, flick over my mouth and, for a second, I think he might resist.

But then he steps in, wraps his arm around my waist and pulls me flush against him. Our lips meet.

And the world falls away.

The crowd cheers. But I barely hear them. Because Ashon's kiss isn't gentle. Or staged.

It's possessive and demanding and punishing.

And worse… I kiss him back. Probably because I wish to give him a taste of his own medicine, I tell myself. That he deserves to feel a little bit of his shaken bewilderment I feel. And because memory flares with the reminder that he'd fallen under my spell that night, regardless of the inexperience I brought to his bed. Or perhaps because of it. After all, didn't men like him thump their chests at being the ones to master their bed partners? Fuck their conquests to oblivion?

I'm drowning in sensation, in memory, in the way his mouth moves like he's been waiting to do this for days. Maybe longer.

It's not until his hand skims too low, too intimately, that I pull away.

The applause crashes over us like a wave.

We bow and smile. And at the very first opportunity, I pull my fingers from his and retreat.

Inside the palace, everything is quieter. Dimmer. But my pulse is louder than ever.

It's only as I'm approaching my bedroom door that I realise that Ashon is following me to the bridal wing. God, he's really like the predator he referred himself to.

And simply because I refuse to be prey, I go on the offensive. 'I'll pay you back for that,' I murmur, breath still ragged from the kiss he stole. Or maybe the one I gave back far too willingly.

His smile is lethal and assured, but his eyes are anything but amused. 'Look forward to it, *wife*.'

The word scrapes something raw inside me. Not because it's a lie, but because just now it didn't feel like one. Not entirely.

My skin still buzzes from the way he touched me in front of all those people. From the way I responded, melting into it like I had no pride, no memory, no plan. Like I didn't know exactly what kind of man he was. *Is*.

I fold my arms, trying to contain the tremor that's started in my chest. 'Still believe everything's gone your way?' I ask because I need to reclaim some footing. Because my heart is still galloping and my body is still betraying me.

His smile turns sharp, his tone even sharper. 'You're wearing my ring, the clothes I bought you, sleeping in my house, and now carrying the very name you claimed to despise. And all it's going to cost me is a few hundred acres of land, barely a dent, that I won't even miss once I hand it over? I'm very happy to call that checkmate to me.'

I don't flinch. I've spent my whole life preparing for worse men than him.

'At least I'm doing it for something that matters,' I say, voice quiet but steady. 'For my baby. For my family. What are you doing it for, Ashon? Another headline? More fame? More fortune?'

The smile falters. Only a fraction, but it's enough.

Beneath all the polish and swagger, I hit something.

A nerve.

He doesn't answer right away. He stares at me, dark eyes unreadable, like he's seeing too much and not enough at once. His jaw tightens. A muscle ticks in his cheek. But when he finally speaks, his voice is measured.

'For appearances,' he says, his voice low, his face unreadable, 'we should talk about a honeymoon. A very public, very far-away one.'

I raise an eyebrow. 'You're here to build a movie studio, Ashon. Let's not pretend you have time to lounge on beaches and pretend we like each other.'

His smirk is bitter. 'Ah. So you're afraid of being alone with me?'

'I'm not afraid of you,' I lie. 'Of anything.'

He steps closer, one hand braced on the doorframe above my head. 'Could've fooled me. Every time I touch you, you flinch. Every time you look at me, your pupils blow wide. You're terrified of what's still between us.'

I look away. 'I just don't want to repeat mistakes.'

His laugh is sharp. 'Sure. Let's call it a mistake.' There's a beat of silence, thick and charged. Then he shakes his head. 'A very beautiful mistake. Enough to convince an ordinary man not to look beneath the surface.'

I glance at him, seeing the trap lurking in his eyes. 'Since we both know you believe yourself to be extraordinary, whatever this is...don't.'

'I mean it. I have to hand it to you, you've played the role quite convincingly.'

'That doesn't change anything.'

He jaw tightens. 'Indeed. No need to drive the point home, wife.'

He starts to turn away, but I stop him with a hand on his wrist. And I know the words I'm about to say next are as much a warning drawn in the sand for me as they are for him. 'I meant what I said, Ashon. No intimacy. No lies. No love.'

His mouth curls, cruel and knowing. 'Watch it my dear, you're fast approaching "doth protest too much" territory.' He spins on his heel, then pauses. 'I'll see you downstairs for the next scene. And when Renée gets in touch with potential honeymoon destinations, don't dawdle. Remember, unless and until I get what I want, your own needs will be equally denied.'

His words are meant to remind me of the land, the studio, the stakes. But they land somewhere else entirely. Lower, deeper. Like he's talking about hunger. Mine. His. *Ours.*

For a beat, as I watch his formidable form stalk away, I forget why I should hate him.

Then I lift my chin, shut the door and remind myself exactly what's at risk if I don't.

And no, it's not just the land. Not just the deed that should've been passed down with my mother's love and my father's faith.

But the part of me I haven't let anyone touch since that night in his LA mansion. The part that stupidly, stupidly believed there might've been more to Ashon Biney than power and prestige.

Because I'd thought I sensed it that night beneath his flawless black jacket the night he returned from his mother's funeral. I'd heard the crack in his voice when he'd murmured, 'She's gone,' like it was the first time he'd allowed himself to acknowledge his loss. The first time he'd accepted he was human and could feel pain like the rest of us.

And I should've walked away. Should've offered condolences and slipped out into the hallway like the professional albeit with a hidden purpose. But I didn't.

Instead, I stayed. Let my fingertips press into the back of his neck. Let him kiss me like he was drowning and I was the shore. Let a single moment of human comfort unfold into a night of tangled limbs and whispered nothings that felt too close to hidden desires.

And what haunts me isn't just the sex—though God knows it left an imprint—but the way it felt like a surrender. Like falling into something I'd been craving since the moment I stepped into his house.

That night nearly wrecked me. Because, for a breathless, traitorous moment, I thought maybe I'd used him too for those desires I didn't even know I craved until I was beneath him, sobbing with pleasure.

Which is why I can never risk going back there.

Because I sense that this time, if I fall again, I might not have anything left to bargain with.

Ashon

I married her today, my fake fiancée.

The woman who promised hell on behalf of her family

for a mere thousand acres of her family land. It would be almost laughable if a part of me didn't grudgingly admire the fierceness with which she fought for those she cared about. If it didn't remind me that with my own father gone, there was someone left to fight for me. If I needed it.

Which I don't.

A lesser man would reel at the twists and turns of this particular movie. It's a good thing then I'm well versed in the art of keeping an audience gripped. My smile tastes bitter because of course this is *my life*, not a fucking movie.

And this particular scene? It's verging on the pathetic.

Because it's nearly midnight and I'm alone in my father's old study, surrounded by half-drunk whisky and blueprints for a dream I'm beginning to wonder if I can still afford—emotionally, at least. The irony isn't lost on me.

My wedding night and I'm in here working, while my bride—my infuriating, too-beautiful, *pregnant* bride—is down the hall behind a locked door.

Under different circumstances, we'd be in that room together. Naked. Tangled in sheets. She'd still be gasping my name. I'd be buried deep inside her, chasing the way she clenched when I told her not to stop saying please.

The way she never did, not once that night. The memories are too vivid. Too fucking dangerous. Because they weren't supposed to mean anything.

And yet…

I push back from the desk, every muscle in my jaw clenched tight. I should hate her. I want to. The way she baited me. Played her hand like a pro, held back the truth about that damn land until she could use it as leverage.

I hear her voice in my head again, all faux-innocence and outrage. *'It was a cocoa farm. My father's livelihood. My mother's pride. My childhood.'*

Naturally, I had my people research that claim in the days after her revelation. Quietly. And when it came back with several sharp grains of truth, I asked Nana about the acquisition. He'd barely looked up from his morning papaya and coffee. *'I don't remember who owed me what. If that tenant had paid their dues, maybe they wouldn't have lost the land. That's business, Ashon. You can't get sentimental about every sob story.'*

I hadn't told him why I was asking. I didn't want him to know she'd gotten under my skin.

Or that she still is.

And dammit, it chafes greatly that her words, her reference to her mother's pride, should excavate my own memories.

Now I can't stop thinking about my father. About what he sacrificed so I could realise my own dream, repeatedly going toe to toe with his own father, even when Nana would've burned the country down to save face from the purported disgrace I was bringing to the Biney name.

My father didn't live to see the legacy I'm trying to build. But this studio? It's for him. All of it. Every concrete slab, every sleepless night, every goddamn compromise.

And now that I'm going to be a father…this dream on the cusp of reality feels more imperative than ever.

I scrub a hand down my face and set my jaw in stone. There's no option of backing out. I *have* to finish what I started.

I leave the study. My body is restless and overheated, the kind that requires liquor or a cold shower.

My brain's jammed with figures, architectural projections, budget approvals—anything to keep my focus off the fact that there's a woman down the hall carrying my child. A woman I kissed in front of half of Ghana. A woman I can't stop thinking about.

I told myself I agreed to this arrangement because it would give us space. Boundaries. Keeping a crotchety and cunning old man onside long enough to fulfil a dream. But I'm beginning to wonder if I'm not stoking the beginnings of a nightmare.

The estate is dark, hushed, save for the low rumble of the generator and the occasional chirp of a gecko clinging to the outside walls. Moonlight spills through the windows, turning the marble floors silver. A soft breeze hums through the open shutters, but it's not enough to cool the heat under my skin.

I drift into the kitchen…another kitchen, telling myself I'm only here for cold water. Maybe something stronger. Maybe even some sign that what started in my kitchen in Bel Air wasn't as monumental as I'm making it out to be.

But then I hear the sound.

The door clicks open. And even before she appears, I know it's her. From the way my skin jumps. The way my chest and throat tighten. Hell, the way my cock jerks in my pants.

Cilla.

She moves like a whisper—barefoot, silk robe clinging to her curves like it was made for my undoing. Her hair's loose, a wild halo that catches the moonlight. She doesn't see me at first, reaching for a mango on the island like she's done it a hundred times before.

But when she looks up, our eyes lock.

She goes still, almost as still as I am. The air thickens with that infernal inescapable chemistry designed just for us—two people who shouldn't crave each other but do.

She's glowing in a way she wasn't a week ago. It's not the pregnancy. It's something sharper. More dangerous. The kind of glow that comes when a woman knows her power and refuses to let it be tamed. The kind of strength and spirit that in another time and place I would've—

No. *Absolutely not.*

'You're not sleeping,' I say, my voice low, rougher than I mean it to be. Spouting inane words that should shame me, a notable master of dialogue and nuance.

She lifts a brow, not exactly mocking but not benign either. The bracing before the unleashing, maybe. 'Neither are you.'

I take a breath and cross the room slowly. Deliberate. Her eyes track me the whole way.

My sweats hang low, waistband slung lazily across my hips, dipping with the weight of my body's reaction to this woman.

To my wife.

I'm aware of her gaze skimming me, just as I'm aware of the way the silk moulds to her breasts, the soft curve of her stomach already faint beneath it.

I glance at her belly. Then at her mouth.

'You should be resting.'

'I'm pregnant, not incapacitated,' she says, tone even and careful but tired. There's something fragile in the way she leans against the counter, like she's more worn down than she's willing to admit.

A beat of silence stretches between us. I breach the distance and pluck the mango from her hand. She's too surprised to react or maybe she's waiting for me to pick up the knife so she can locate hers. My lips twitch.

'Something funny?'

'Not if I find a way to turn the prospect of being stabbed on my wedding night into a comedy.'

She blinks long and lush eyelashes at me, then frowns. But I see the faintest twitch curve one corner of her sensual mouth.

'So is this a pregnancy craving or just a run-of-the-mill midnight snack on your wedding night?'

Something gleams in her eyes, and her gaze moves over me once more, lingering on where it shouldn't. Or rather where it absolutely should, were this an age-old dance to the glorious inevitable. Sadly a very virile part of my anatomy is eager for it to be the latter.

'Does it need to be one or the other?'

'Oh yes, wife. Because you don't strike me as the spur of the moment type.'

I keep my tone even, despite the churning of new and old revelations between us, because—I tell myself—the day has been festooned with enough acrimony and even the devil needs a break. And perhaps she feels the same because she blinks again but doesn't spit fire at me the way I know she should.

'You don't know me that well, Ashon.' It's a firm admonishing. Perhaps a touch reluctant, even.

A well-brought up boy, like I am, enjoying the Ivy League entrapments should cross the room and fetch a plate to serve her on. But I'm in no mood to vacate this bubble. Damn if I want to prematurely disrupt this and be forced back into the study to do work that can wait. So I slice a plump piece of mango and offer it to her on the flat of the knife.

Then I ask what I probably shouldn't. 'Do you think about it? That night?' Her lips part. A flicker of shock—or want—flares in her eyes before she masks it. I step closer. 'Because I do,' I say. 'More than I should. How it started. And how it ended.' I mean to study her, watch for a reaction. Perhaps even a sign of remorse for how this played out, something Delphine never displayed.

And then I kick myself. For wishing it in the first place and for comparing the two women. They might not be as different as night and day, but yes, they're closer to dawn and dusk. Both had agendas. But, so far, my wife has stuck to her insistence of not wanting a penny more than was initially agreed on top of the return of her family land. She signed the pre-nup with a pointed flourish after a cursory perusal. And, as much as I hated to admit it, that move had surprised me. Seared its ungrasping significance into my memory in a way that made her just that little bit more unforgettable.

As if I could forget this stunning creature, half-glaring at me with nostrils flared.

'Stop it.' Firmer. Less reluctant. But still bristling with heat and sensuality this night, this moment deserves. If only…

And those two words draw my brow up, comfort and habit demanding sardonicism. 'We agreed on no intimacy.' I pause, holding her gaze. 'But you didn't say no memories. Sometimes, isn't that all that sustains us? What makes us pick our next steps with better care?'

She stiffens. Her fingers dig into the piece of mango like it might keep her upright. I'm closer now. Close enough to feel the heat rolling off her. Her nipples press lightly against the silk, pebbling beneath it. My mouth dries.

I reach up. Gently, slowly, I brush a stray braid off her cheek. It's barely a touch. But it crackles like fire.

'Do you remember,' I murmur, striving to contain heavy things that strained to come out, 'how you said my name when you came?'

Her throat works. She swallows hard. Her thighs clench. I see it in the flicker of movement, the subtle shift of weight. I know that look. I know that need.

She steps back a mere half-step as if her body is resisting the distance. 'What are you doing?' She mutters, then shakes her head. 'Don't answer that. Because what I remember is how fast you thought the worst of me. Ensured I would be punished for giving you what we both wanted.'

The words hit like a gut punch. Not enough to damage but enough to remind me of my power, and the overexertion of it. It grates to admit it, but I might have been a little too heavy-handed in my sorrow. There was crime, certainly but the punishment didn't fit. At least not then…

And now?

I shake my head. 'Cilla—'

'This is a contract,' she says. Her voice is cool, but I hear the tremor beneath. 'Let's not rewrite it with hormones and fantasy.'

She turns, stops at the sink long enough to rinse the juice off her fingers. Then she walks away.

The scent of mango and hibiscus lingers. A bead of juice drips from the counter to the floor.

I stare after her.

And I burn with want that shouldn't exist and yet *does*. And with the distinct notion that I might have met the only woman on the face of this earth who might well step up to, and perhaps even attempt to, slay a Biney.

She won't succeed of course, but the process of watching her try is…intriguing.

CHAPTER FIVE

Cilla

IN THE DAYS that follow, I completely despise myself for dwelling on those moments in the kitchen. Dear God, what it is with me and Ashon Biney and kitchens? Even worse, I hate that I walked away because all I returned to was more tossing and turning, but wildly infested with Ashon's low, deep voice when he enquired if I *'think about that night...because I do. More than I should.'*

Meaning what? He hates himself for it? Or it's a delicious, decadent memory he can't help but revisit, almost as fervently as I do?

God. Enough.

It's almost a relief when Renée calls three mornings after the wedding, efficient as always—even from another continent.

'We're shortlisting three locations for the honeymoon,' she starts, the choices a foregone conclusion because of course they are. I curb the need to object for the sake of it.

'Have you?' I murmur, feeling a touch of catty satisfaction when she hesitates for a moment. 'And when is all this happening or is that to be a happy surprise?'

'In the next week, two at most, if that's all right?'

I curb a snort, bite my tongue against a snarky retort about whether that matters since I seem to be secondary to decisions about me. 'Sure, why not,' I say instead.

'Great. We've settled on Cap Ferrat, Seychelles or a boutique wildlife lodge in Botswana. Unless you object?'

I'm still blinking sleep from my eyes, curled on the terrace with a mango smoothie Ashon insisted I drink. I'm not entirely sure whether he's capitalising on my craving for mangoes to make some sort of point or he's being thoughtful for the sake of the child I'm carrying. Whatever. The air is heavy with humidity and a heady swirl of hibiscus from the garden below. And I can easily take another half-hour nap.

'Cap Ferrat?' I echo.

'It's on the French Riviera.' Before I reply that I'm well aware of the location, she continues, 'He filmed *The Heir Apparent* there, the movie that made him a household name. The terrace scene overlooking the sea? That wasn't a set. That was the villa he stayed in for months during filming.' Renée pauses, then says more softly, 'It meant a lot to him. First time he said he felt seen.'

I'm not sure why that sticks with me.

Or why it settles something strange in my chest.

Because I'm not supposed to care. I shouldn't be chasing meaning in a sea of illusions. This is strategy. Nothing more.

But when I call Renée back two hours later, I choose Cap Ferrat.

'Excellent choice, Mrs Biney. No need to pack much, we'll have a brand new wardrobe awaiting your arrival.'

And that…was that.

Until breakfast the next morning.

Ashon barely touches his toast, instead reaching for the cutlets of mango. It's become a thing now, sharing mango with him at breakfast.

He's dressed down for once, crisp white shirt rolled at the sleeves, collar open. He still manages to look like a luxury brand come to life.

'I heard you picked Cap Ferrat.' His tone is even. But his eyes? Sharper than usual. Digging for something?

I shrug. 'I liked the sound of it.'

His brow lifts, mouth tilting at one corner. 'Sentimental choice for someone so committed to emotional detachment.'

I slice a mango with unnecessary precision. 'You assume sentiment. I'm just yearning for a break from the heat.'

We sit with the lie for the moment, and yes, I avoid his incisive eyes while he takes a sip of his coffee.

'I also gave Renée a backup. Somewhere quieter. More… grounded. Somewhere on your bucket list.'

I glance up, hating the lurch of my heart. 'Oh…you did?'

He nods. 'Botswana. You once mentioned it to your uncle in passing—he told me at the engagement lunch, I think—that you dreamed of visiting the Okavango Delta. Something about your mother showing you a photo in a National Geographic map when you were little.'

I freeze. The ache of that memory, her voice, tracing the river with her finger, the way she whispered, *I wanted to take you there when you were younger but maybe someday, you'll see it yourself.*

My uncle mentioning it to Ashon is one surprising thing but… 'You remember that from a fleeting meeting?' I ask, because I know how much Ashon spent with each guest, hell, *aware of him*, period, the same way I'm aware of a dancing cobra—with a worrying, near hypnotic fascination.

He shrugs. 'I listen. Sometimes. When it suits me.'

Something flutters low in my stomach. Nerves. Or maybe

something worse. Emotional elation. 'Well we'll see. Maybe. Let's not get ahead of ourselves.'

'Indeed. But one unavoidable thing is the ultrasound.' He fixes me with a steady stare, glances down at his Richard Mille watch, then nods at my plate. 'Eat up, wife. We don't want to be late to see our child for the first time.'

Despite the ultra private hospital status of our destination, the room is warm, too bright. White walls. The faint scent of antiseptic seemingly unavoidable in places like this.

A machine beeps in the background as the doctor smooths cool gel across my lower belly.

I flinch at the temperature and before I can steel myself, Ashon's hand finds mine.

Like magnets, my eyes are drawn to his face and I swallow when I see this is not for show. There's no audience here. No Nana, no paparazzi, no agenda. Just us and this sterile room. I should pull away but I don't.

Because right then the sound fills the room, instantly reaching for my heart, capturing it.

A flutter. Then a thrum. Then something steady and impossibly alive.

My baby's heartbeat.

I suck in a breath. My head whips towards the monitor, but it's immediately drawn back to the man whose breath has also caught. Ashon's already looking at me, his eyes dark and wide with something I can't name. A little awe. Perhaps joy. It's indefinable but it's there. Something raw and reverent and real.

His grip tightens around mine. His thumb brushes over my knuckles in a slow, anchoring sweep. I feel the pressure in my throat, tears I didn't know I was holding pressing behind my eyes. A shared moment I didn't expect and really…

shouldn't hang on to, but there it is. Joining the cons list of everything I shouldn't have done or craved where this man is concerned.

This man. The father of the blob squirming about on the screen.

Dear God...

The doctor smiles kindly. 'There's your little one. Strong heartbeat and growing right on track. With a healthy diet and exercise regime I won't need to see you for another six weeks.'

The screen flickers with the grainy black-and-white image—small limbs, curved spine, tiny movements. It hits me with full force. That's my baby. *Ours*, I amend, even in my mind because I can't fool myself that its father isn't fully intent on claiming him or her.

Ashon leans forward slightly. I see his jaw clench, see the muscle twitch there. Like he's holding himself together too tightly. Like if he lets go, something irreversible will happen.

'I—' I start, but don't finish. There are no words big enough for this.

Then the moment cracks.

'Oh,' the doctor says lightly, tapping the keyboard, 'your grandfather mentioned he'd like a copy of the scan image for the family archives. I'll print three.'

'No,' Ashon says sharply.

The doctor blinks. 'Pardon?' A trace of apprehension, perhaps belatedly realising that while Nana Biney might be the ruler of this pride, he's very quickly aging out.

'You'll print two. One for my wife. One for me. That's all.' His tone is cool, firm. Final. 'Is that understood?'

'Yes. Of course, sir.'

As the doctor hurries to finalise the procedure, I blink at him, yet another emotion I don't want to feel moving through me. Because it wasn't the refusal but the implacable force with which he countermanded his grandfather's wish. Like this—this heartbeat, this image—isn't for public display. Or even an old man's roughshod demand. It's sacred. *Ours.*

And he wants it to remain just ours.

I look away quickly, covering the rush of heat in my chest. I shouldn't be thrilled. I shouldn't let it matter.

But it does.

Done, the doctor clears her throat delicately, sensing tension and quickly moving on. The rest of the appointment is all protocol and scheduling.

But Ashon doesn't let go of my hand.

Even when we step back out into the waiting room and a pair of eager, meddling cousins from the Biney side pretend not to pounce on us with curious eyes and sly smiles, he draws me in closer, his palm warm on the small of my back. His other hand reaches for my fingers again.

'My dear, are you taking your folic acid?' Auntie Paulina demands.

'You must stop carrying heavy things,' another pipes in. 'Don't lift even your purse!'

Ashon takes my bag smoothly off my shoulder, a tight smile that fools no one curving his lips. 'There. Crisis averted. I'm going to take my wife home now. The honeymoon isn't going to celebrate itself.'

He smiles down at me, eyes sparkling and a far too sensual mouth curved with wicked promise and heaven help me, mine curves back before I can caution myself of exactly what this is.

In public, we're supposed to be a couple in love.

But as Nana's driver whisks us away in an air-conditioned cocoon, and my hand rests protectively over my still-flat stomach—uncaring that Ashon watches the motion and says nothing—I wonder, foolishly if just for a minute…it doesn't feel like pretending.

Cilla

Two weeks later

I'm arranging flowers when the Biney butler approaches me.

'A call for you, madam.'

I look up, a little surprised, more than a little alarmed. My mother, uncle and my cousin Tessa, the three people I'm closest to and speak to more often that anyone else, have my mobile number but my phone is currently sitting in my pocket.

'Who is it?'

'I believe it's the Land Registrar General, madam.'

I'm not sure why my heart jumps into my throat as I take the phone. 'Hello?' My voice displays more than a shade of wariness.

'Mrs Rockson-Biney, thanks for taking the call. I've been trying to reach your husband but I've been unsuccessful.'

'What's this about?'

'The land at Nkyinkyim. We've been asked to delay finalising the transfer until Mr Ashon Biney confirms his authorisation. I'm afraid we can't proceed until then. Do you know when that will be?'

I stand straighter, the long bougainvillea stem in my hand snapping. 'I'm sorry, what do you mean *delay*? Wasn't everything submitted and signed?' I have no idea what I'm talking about but I'll bluff my way to the truth if necessary. Because that continued lurching in my heart? It's a warning system I can't deny. It reeks of the same dread I felt in the pit of my stomach that day when I heard my father pleading with Nana Biney's lawyers. Dread that came to pass.

Surely Ashon wouldn't—

'Yes, ma'am. But the authorisation for release has been put on hold. Just temporarily, I'm sure. These things happen all the time but we wanted to confirm that this was indeed authorised by your husband and for how long.'

'Thank you,' I say, managing, barely, to keep my voice even. Calm. 'Before you go, can you tell me, is there any reason the delay will be necessary? Any problems with the transfer?'

He clears his throat, hesitates for a moment. 'Not on our side, madam. We've dealt with the Bineys in the past. He likes a smooth and swift transaction and we've ensured this is in place this time too. I suppose that's why I was surprised when we got the message about the pause.'

My heart thuds, dull and heavy, as if it doesn't want to believe the words ringing their warning. That I was foolish to take his promise and a mere signed paper on face value. That somewhere deep inside I'd hoped beyond even the land that should be first and foremost in my thought, that the father of the child I'm carrying wouldn't revert to family type. 'I see. We...we'll get back to you on that.'

These things happen all the time...

Of course they do.

Just not to *me*.

Not when I've already paid in flesh and vow and blood.

I hang up and hand the phone to the hovering butler.

I don't scream. Not until he's gone and I've abandoned the flowers and gone up the stairs and shut my bedroom door behind me.

Not until I enter my dressing room and I sink to my knees on the carpeted floor, press my forehead into the row of folded linen and muslin, and scream into the silence until my throat burns and my ribs ache.

He agreed.

I...trusted him, perhaps not wholeheartedly—because my heart wasn't quite that foolish an organ—but in the belief that he would let this thing that means far more to me than it would ever mean to him, form the foundation of…something.

And as I blink back hot tears, I know that's what sears the most. I'd unwittingly lowered the ramparts of my guard.

And, he…what? He's turning it into a leash. A golden chain he can display like a prize and like counter-leverage?

When I finally pull myself together, I find him in the east wing office, shirt rolled up to the elbows, his desk strewn with script notes and architectural plans for the new studio.

The one thing he's unwavering about, everything else be damned, right?

He looks up, surprised but not a shade of guilt in sight. That hurts more than I expect.

'Cilla,' he says my name with that bite of authority he does with everything, but his gaze is already dropping to my belly as if my existence only matters in the seed growing in my womb. Another thing he's taken to doing lately. Another thing he's unwaveringly possessive about.

That shouldn't count or hurt, especially not since the phone call. And yet…

'Is everything all right?'

I force a nod. 'Got a call from the land registrar.'

Ashon nods absently, but I catch the hint of stiffening in his shoulders as he flips a page. 'Probably just bureaucracy. They move slower than a funeral procession.'

I step forward. 'They said the process was *delayed* until you confirm. Is that true?'

That gets his attention. He sets the paper down. 'It's a few more checks, Cilla. I just need to sign off. Haven't had the time.'

'You've had *weeks*.' Weeks during which I'm ashamed to say have been filled with planning for motherhood, wondering about what kind of mother I'll be and a slow burning hope of rekindling my freelance documentary career than in thinking about the reparations I should've been pushing for my family.

His gaze narrows slightly. 'I've had a studio to build and projects that need my attention. An unexpected marriage to plan.' His eyes drop to my belly again. 'And now a new legacy to protect.' He shrugs his broad shoulders. 'I'm all-powerful, I admit, but even the Almighty took a breather.' There's an attempt at humour, but it emerges tight, his eyes far too watchful. Too calculating. 'Besides, what's the hurry?'

I take a breath. Swallow the sting. 'You wouldn't happen to be playing me, would you? Stringing me along now you've got your ring on my finger?'

Something flickers in his eyes—guilt or affront, I can't tell. 'I said I'd take care of it.'

'That's not the same. But, know this, if you do intend to play me, you'll spend a very long time regretting it.'

'And you should know, I don't react very well to threats. So put your claws away, dear wife, before I call your bluff just to see how effective your fireworks truly are.'

I hold my ground, even though my pulse betrays me with a reckless leap. 'You think this is a game? Some extended noir scene you get to cut to suit the ending you want?'

'Not quite. Because unlike you, I'm still enjoying the opening scenes of this epic. While you seem to want to race to the credits. Why is that?' Dark brown eyes pierce me.

And my breath catches.

Because his words shouldn't matter. But they do far too much. And it terrifies me how easily he slices through my practiced detachment, how deeply that line lands.

I came here angry. I should still be angry. But beneath that, I think I was hoping—naively, stupidly—that he might soothe some of the hurt from the phone call. That he might say one thing to make me believe this isn't all just calculation.

I square my shoulders. Lie with my spine if I have to. 'I'm not racing anywhere. But maybe I've seen enough of your "epic" to know how it ends.'

He doesn't reply. Just watches me, his lips pursed and narrows his eyes in silent condemnation. But that too, isn't an answer.

And that silence plants the first real crack in the ground beneath us.

I nod slowly, like I've heard what I needed to, even though I haven't.

Then I leave before I say something I can't take back.

Before I confess how much my chest hurts when my heart should absolutely not be in this dangerous game.

Ashon

She doesn't speak to me at dinner.

She greets Nana with sweet, composed courtesy, folds herself gracefully into her seat, and smiles like she's starring in a political campaign, not sitting next to the man she married out of necessity. Not the man who decided to pump the brakes on simply handing over the means by which his new wife could leave him, despite their year's agreement. A man who isn't even entirely sure why he made that decision when he had a veritable army of attorneys both here and in the US to ensure nothing is done against his wishes.

But… I'd meant it when I asked what the hurry was. And I'd waited with more than an alarming knot of tension inside me.

Now the silence between us ticks like a deliberate time bomb. Chilly.

I try to ignore it, digging into the fufu and palm nut soup like it's a distraction instead of punishment. But I feel her. Every shift of her body. Every breath she doesn't aim in my direction. Every inch of skin under that soft burgundy dress that refuses to even brush against me.

Nana eyes us both with sharp, unrelenting interest.

'So,' he says, settling deeper into his chair. 'Have we settled on names yet? Something strong. Ancestral. The press will want to know. *I* want to know.'

I stare into my soup like it might offer an escape route. Cilla, poised as ever, lifts her water glass and smiles without warmth.

'We plan to discuss it,' she says. 'I have a few options I'm considering.'

I glance sideways at her, inwardly grimacing at the single loosened knot, knowing it's because of her. Her grudging attention. *We?*

Nana frowns. 'It's a joint decision, child.'

'Of course,' she replies sweetly, 'but the child is in *my* body, so I reserve the right to veto any name that makes it sound like I gave birth to an oil tycoon or a dead coloniser.'

That earns a huff of laughter from Nana and a tightening in my chest.

Because even angry, she's luminous. The rest of the meeting progresses, Nana probably satisfied with the blood-stirring skirmish. I let their conversation flow over me as I try *not* to ponder the true motives behind my action. Try *not* to consider that there might be a hint of desperation lurking in there somewhere.

After dessert—mango and pineapple compote—Cilla rises without a word.

I stand, instinctively, ready to offer her my arm.

She doesn't look at me. Doesn't wait. Just sweeps out of the room like a queen leaving a court that no longer amuses her.

A minute later, I hear the door down the east wing close.

Then the silence.

I rake a hand through my hair. The chair creaks under my weight when I slump back into it.

'She's angry,' Nana says casually, sipping his after-dinner brandy. 'Care to share why?'

'She's tired,' I mutter. 'And no I won't be discussing my wife with you.'

'Hmm. Beware of a woman's silences. Those are more lethal than a screaming shrew.'

I clench my jaw. 'I don't need your advice, *paapa*. Especially on a topic that's none of your business.'

Nana leans forward, voice low and sharp. 'You brought her here. You married her. You put my family name in her womb and made her the centre of a very public circus. So don't talk to me about what *isn't* my business.'

'She knew what she was getting into,' I snap.

He barks a laugh. 'No one ever does, Ashon. Not with us.'

My temples throb. I push my chair back and rise. 'I'm not discussing this with you.'

'You don't trust her,' he says simply.

I stop. My spine straightens.

'I don't trust *anyone*,' I say. 'And you taught me that.'

Nana stares at me for a long moment, then nods slowly. 'Good. And I pray to God that boy or girl in her belly does the same. The only ones we can truly rely on in this life is ourselves.'

I leave him sitting there, brandy in hand, watching me like a man who sees a mirror walking away.

In my wing, the lights are dimmed. The hallway hums with night. But my head refuses to quiet. It's full of doubts and her eyes are full of fire.

But the one thing I can admit, as I tear off my clothes and

step into a cool shower, is that, deep in my marrow, that I want Cilla. Still.

Not the version I can control through my lawyers or predict. Not even the convenient wife on paper or the grasping gold-digger I erroneously convinced myself she was. The one easily used and then discarded with relief and barely a thought that didn't exist after all.

I want the real woman, the one who cut me with her raw sensuality and open, unsullied comfort that night, who kissed like it cost her something precious, who now throws my name back at me like a pesky nuisance where other cower in sycophancy.

It should feel absurd that I crave the woman who wants nothing from me save what she is owed but that niggle of thoughts grows with alarming speed.

And wanting her terrifies me more than any deal, any investor, any legacy.

Because I could survive losing all of that.

But when even the slightest hint of her attaining leverage over me tightens a vice in my chest? I need to drill down into that, sooner rather than later. So I can deal with it properly.

Even if I hate that a part of me knows exactly what is behind my questionable feelings.

A reason that might stray very close to…obsession with the very woman I shouldn't crave this much.

Cilla

The coastline of Cap Ferrat glitters like something out of a dream.

Even through the tinted windows of the Rolls-Royce, the Mediterranean winks beneath the sun, impossibly blue, the villas carved into the cliffs like something from a luxury travel reel. I press a hand to my belly as we glide past them—palms swaying lazily, flowers spilling from balconies, salt on the breeze.

For the first time in weeks, I breathe free and deep.

No Nana. No probing eyes. No staged smiles or hushed arguments behind closed doors. Just clean air and the sound of ocean spray licking the rocky shore.

Ashon, seated beside me, watches the world like he owns it. Like he's brought me here not just for the performance, but for the promise it implies.

I glance down one last time at the text exchange with my cousin Tessa.

Tessa: Sorry I missed the wedding. Long story. But you owe me photos, cousin.

Me: You were missed. But I get it. You hate all things love and lace these days.

Tessa: I hate anything that smells like a trap. Speaking of… what's going on, Cilla? Really. Don't give me the PR version.

Me: It's…complicated.

Tessa: You're married to a Biney. I can smell the complication from three time zones away. Just…don't let him get under your skin.

Me: You sound like you speak from experience? Anything you want to tell me?

Tessa: It's…complicated. But listen, whatever made you do this, the Biney's are cunning. And, I know you don't want my interference, but don't expect me to sit on my hands if things look sketchy. If I think you need protecting—I'll act. And don't tell me not to. You'd do the same for me.

Me: Always. I'm fine, Tess. Just trying to make smart choices.

Tessa: Make the smartest one: think twice before you trust a man who weaves dreams and magic into box office billions.

The warning within has a bolstering effect but also terrifies me because while I'm humbled to know she has my back I'm thrown by how much I want her to be wrong.

I push it all away as the villa comes into view. Of course it's breathtaking—stone and glass sprawling across a hilltop with panoramic views. There's a helipad, a terraced infinity pool, a team of staff waiting in sleek uniforms. I force myself not to gape.

As we step inside, Ashon rattles off a list of things Renée's arranged—sunset yacht tours, a private chef who does prenatal-friendly meals, a spa retreat tucked into a lavender grove.

'Does she pick your underwear too?' I say before I can stop myself. It's flippant. Bitter. Petty, even. But I don't walk it back.

His jaw tenses, but not with anger. 'Renée's been with me a long time,' he says quietly. 'Since the beginning. She got me through losing my father. Then my mother. And everything that came after.' He pauses, eyes on the horizon beyond the glass doors. 'When you've spent your whole life being wanted for what you can give, not who you are, you learn to trust loyalty over emotion.' His voice drops, rougher now. Harder. 'People tend to let you down so it's always best to keep them out.'

Guilt prickles. I glance away. 'I didn't mean—'

'It's fine,' he says. 'You're not the only one with armour, Cilla.'

We stand there for a beat, surrounded by too much space and unspoken things. The silence thickens until he adds, voice low, 'About that night. After…'

I look up, startled.

'I could've handled it differently. You walking away… I took it personally.'

'I know,' I whisper. 'It felt intensely personal. And not at all in a good way.'

His eyes search mine for something I'm not ready to give. For forgiveness. Can I risk it? Especially when the battering of my foundations seems incessant and relentless? I hold my breath, caught between reassurance and hanging onto my grievance.

Then he nods. Just once. And the moment slips away and I'm not sure whether I'm relieved or sorry.

'I have a few calls to make. Call for refreshments if you need, otherwise I'll see you for dinner at seven?' he says, eyebrows raised.

I nod because what else can I do?

And he leaves.

Dinner is served on the terrace, the sun bleeding into the horizon in streaks of blush and gold, like the sky itself can't bear to say goodbye. The villa glows in the soft amber light, every surface kissed with warmth and luxury—silverware glinting and linen rippling in the ocean breeze, the scent of grilled sea bass and citrus lingering between us.

We sit across from each other at a table set for intimacy, low candles flickering, crystal catching the last of the sun's gleam, white roses spilling from a silver bowl.

It's quiet, almost too quiet, but the tension that usually

brims between us has mellowed into something...less rigid. A truce, maybe. Or the fragile beginnings of one. Or it could all be wishful thinking on my part and we'll be back to digging furrows in each other to see which one of us bled, *hurt* the most.

Maybe it's this place where he set his masterpiece.

Wow, melodramatic much?

He serves me first, unprompted, his movements fluid and precise, and oh so sexy and assured. I thank him, a little brisker than I intended, perhaps in direct opposition to the softening inside me. But if he objects, he doesn't show it. He merely nods again, eyes unreadable as he lifts his wine glass.

We eat slowly, saying little, but there's something comforting in the silence this time. Like we've both stopped pretending for a moment and are simply existing—two people, on a beautiful terrace, trying to find peace in a war of emotional attrition.

Neither of us feel inclined towards conversation. That feels okay too as we sit there and the sea hushes in the distance like a lullaby.

When we're done eating the most sublime food Ashon stands and comes around to my chair, the perfect gentleman, and we walk side by side along the marbled corridor, past a series of antique mirrors and open archways. That feels extremely fine too.

I expect us to part at the first hallway bend, but instead we keep walking—together—until we reach the far wing.

There are two doors.

One to the left, carved with a soft curve of C for Cilla. The other to the right, darker wood, marked A. Matching brass handles. Matching etched glass above. One shared suite, yes—but separate bedrooms.

Renée's touch, no doubt.

It shouldn't bother me.

It shouldn't spark this strange ache, this hollow little bloom of disappointment in my chest. We've agreed to nothing but civility, strategy and zero intimacy. But still, in hindsight and with calmer temperatures, am I being disingenuous to think he accepted this arrangement too easily? There was no protest, very little hesitation. No regret except maybe on our wedding night when he let that little question slip?

I wonder if that's a good thing. Or the worst possible omen. Or am I protesting too much, as he'd mocked me for?

At the threshold of my room, I pause. So does he.

There's a beat, just a breath between us, where everything stills. Where I feel the weight of his gaze press into me like a hot little secret, itching to come to light and life. Where I think he might step forward. Kiss me. Shatter what's left of our resolve.

But instead, he steps back. His voice is quiet, entirely too composed. The Ashon Biney I know and, yes, maybe loathe a little for this supreme control part of me wants to shatter. '*Bonne nuit*, Mrs Biney.'

I manage a small smile despite feeling a little brittle. 'Goodnight, Ashon.'

I enter and close the door gently, the whisper of it like a sigh between us. My pulse flutters. My body is warm, too warm. Neither of us says what we're really thinking.

Not yet. Maybe never.

Because really, what else but unholy devastation lies in wait for even the tiniest loss in this war between us?

CHAPTER SIX

Ashon

BY SILENT MUTUAL AGREEMENT, probably prompted by that poor excuse for an apology on my part, we settled into an uneasy truce. One day blends into two. Tensions don't ease but they don't exactly strangle.

The sea's gone molten gold under the late afternoon sun, turning everything it touches into cinematic perfection.

And a memory.

I stand at the edge of the terrace, a drink untouched in my hand, watching her, and oh yes, mocking that ever-increasing inability to take my eyes off her. But I am a red-blooded male, after all, and in that white bikini, her wet hair slicked back, droplets racing over her skin and drifting across my pool like without a care seeming care in the world? It's…mesmerising.

My gaze lingers on her flat belly as my other hand slips into my pocket. My fingers find the ultrasound photo. Crumpled at the corners now. In just three days, I've memorised every grainy inch of it. That tiny curve. The ghost of a spine. A pulse that sounded like salvation and the heaviest gauntlet *to do better* wrapped into one.

I should be working. I should be planning.

But instead, I'm remembering.

Cap Ferrat was the last place I came with my father before everything changed. Before the last crutch I wasn't even aware I needed was ripped away.

I didn't understand then but I'm starting to.

The sliding door opens behind me. Bare feet pad across the stone tiles.

Cilla.

She moves like the tide—inevitable, elemental.

I strive to rip myself from the harrowing memories. The impotency of knowing I could do nothing to save the man who gave up everything from me, a man ripped from my life far too soon. *The good die young* had never felt so real as it did then, knowing the best thing to happen to a floundering man who needed guidance was watching the epitome of that goodness lose his battle with life. Bitterness and the injustice of it all rises in my throat but I strive to push it away. To put the game face on that terrifies producers and studio executives alike. 'Do you have a preference on what you want to do tomorrow?'

Her laugh is soft, a deflection before it forms. 'You know, Renée left me a whole list of activities. Wine tastings, even though that's off the table for at least nine months. Helicopter rides. Something about a private art exhibit.'

I turn. She's radiant from the swim, a flush high in her cheeks, lashes wet and sticking together. But her voice has that edge again. Jealousy or pride—I can't tell which. Probably both.

I set my drink down, draw my hand from the picture in my pocket and grab a towel from the chair. I walk to her, shaking it out with a snap. 'Careful there, I see the claws coming out again,' I say, draping the towel around her shoulders. 'Put them away, wife. There's no need for jealousy.'

'I'm not jealous,' she says tartly, tucking the towel tighter. 'I'm just—'

'Let's not do this tonight, hmm?' I cut in, softer than I mean to be. 'It's a beautiful sunset. Let's not spoil it with biting or games.'

She looks up at me. Eyes dark and wary. 'Are you calling me a shrew?'

'I would never be so uncouth.'

She keeps staring, then a sigh escapes. 'I just thought you brought me here to perform again.'

'I brought you here,' I say, carefully, 'because it mattered.'

'To your father? Renée mentioned something…'

She knows.

I pause. Then nod. 'Yes, but to me too.'

That stills her.

She opens her mouth, then closes it. Her hand lifts for a second as if to touch my chest, but she stops short. And maybe it's that slight hesitation that cracks my doors open. That reminds me far too brutally of sublime hours we spent two months ago before the bitter echoes of history repeating itself reared its ugly head. Because whichever way you cut it, she had proved that she did want something.

And while I slot that lesser sin under the heading of label of family and legacy, two things I understand, it didn't negate the fact that I was lonely—no!

Alone. Yes. A formidable island that was the envy of a great many? Indeed.

But *lonely*? Fuck no.

Then why do you crave her touch? And not even entirely sexually? Why do you wish for her to lay that comforting hand on you the way she did that night.

Enough!

I plunge into the story just to get away from the mocking voice echoing relentlessly at the back of my head. 'We were scouting a location. He wasn't well, though he tried to hide it. And then one night, he just collapsed. The diagnosis followed. It was…dire. I wanted us to leave, go back to the States for proper treatment, but he wouldn't. He insisted I stay here, finish my work. So what that his own father was back home, calling him a disappointment because he supported his own son.' My short laugh is caustic, searing. 'We drank wine, watched old movies. He asked me once what I'd do if I had a son. I gave him some arrogant answer. He just smiled and said, "You'll see. Family, whatever form it comes in, is a blessing. Don't forget that".' I glance at her, half-cursing my runaway tongue but also daring her to judge me for this rare crumbling. This diatribe that's tantamount to a third-act breakdown—the kind where the hero, bruised and unravelling, finally confesses everything in the rain and risks it all for the one thing he swore he didn't need. 'But now I guess I do. Because no matter what comes, Cilla, know this. I will claim my child with my last breath.'

She looks at me then, eyes luminous in the gathering dusk. Her breath catches, holds. And, dammit, I feel mine follow, my insides braced to resume our skirmish.

'I believe you,' she says instead, her voice soft but steady.

And I'm nonplussed enough that I can't think of what to say to that.

So I'm silent when she adds, 'And I think he'd be proud of you and what you've achieved.'

Not a platitude or a performance or even a blunted barb. And yet it lands harder than any blow, because for the first time in a long time, I almost believe it.

Silence folds between us again, heavy and full.

Maybe she sways towards me or I do. Whatever it is, it feels instinctual and inevitable as a moon's tide—this draw between us, always pulsing just under the surface.

But we both pull back before contact.

Her breath stutters.

My jaw clenches.

'I… I need to go and change before dinner,' she stammers and turns.

She doesn't see the hand I lift to catch her wrist. To make her stay and just *be* with me—a man who could've sworn only a month ago that he knew himself thoroughly inside and out but now finds his new label of *husband* a wholly unfamiliar fit, and a wife who never asked for the label at all. I might have mastered the art of make-believe but my forays into reality have only unearthed gold diggers, sycophants and women who loved the myth of me more than the man beneath it.

Even my wife, who at this very moment, waits for me to sign on dotted lines that might hasten the end of this…association.

Is that why you're stalling?

I release the growl building in my throat but it does nothing to curb my churning emotions.

And I tell myself that being on my guard and, yes, *stalling* a while is a good thing as I turn and walk in the opposite direction.

But the air we leave behind feels scorched. And I know—without a doubt—we're toeing some invisible line we won't come back from once crossed.

The yacht glides through the cobalt sea, a masterpiece of polished teak and indulgence. Beneath us, the Mediterranean gleams, infinite and deceptive—so beautiful you forget it can drown you with a flippant undercurrent. The breeze is warm against my skin, scented with salt and luxury, and yet I feel like I'm standing on a precipice.

Cilla is at the edge of the deck, her silhouette a study in restraint and rebellion. That white kaftan floats around her like mist and when the sun catches her braids, it looks like the gods themselves threaded gold through them. She hasn't seen me yet. Or maybe she has and she's ignoring me—a specialty she probably has no idea works far better than she knows.

And it *has* been disarming to examine my recent past, then be forced even further back, to discover I don't recall a time I was so actively ignored by a woman. Power and influence has a way of dispensing with every pesky dislike and bad attitude. And yes, even those of women who fool themselves into thinking playing hard to get would spark keener interest when I prefer the cards on the table upfront method.

I slip beside her and let my hand rest lightly on the small of her back. She tenses, just for a second, but doesn't move. I smile intending it to be mocking but it misses the mark and settles on…satisfaction…ease even. I tell myself it's okay, this pretending just for a moment that we're just lovers on a yacht, not actors in a slow-burning war.

'How long does this go on for?' she asks, her grip tight on the railing and on her determination not to look at me. 'The yacht. The touching. The pretending. When does Nana sign over your empire?'

So we can be done with this.

Her voice is flint, striking a spark across the moment. I want to ignore the question. I want to keep looking at her like this, bathed in sunlight, defiant and fucking radiant.

'I don't want to talk about my grandfather right now,' I say, cursing the descent into tension once more.

'Why not?' she murmurs. 'He's the reason we're both here.'

She's right. But it chafes to hear it.

'What would you like?' I say, sarcasm slipping in. 'A midnight confession? Should I bare my soul some more for the sake of ambiance?'

She flinches like I meant to hurt her. I didn't. Not really. But I can't help the bite in my words. I'm tired of being seen as the villain when I'm cut, too. By memory, by the encroaching challenge of fatherhood and the doubt as to whether I'll measure up. Whether what I had with my father can be replicated because something occurred to me last night, as I prowled, restless, down another hallway in another sprawling residence.

He'd had me. But he'd had my mother too. Whereas I have a wife who can't bear to look at me.

She turns to walk away, but I catch her wrist. 'Wait.' She does. And that infernal crack gives, just a little bit more.

'I've been trying to win his approval my entire life, my grandfather,' I say. 'Juilliard. Hollywood. Every red carpet was supposed to prove something. It still wasn't enough.'

I shouldn't be telling her this. But then her face softens and it strikes me then that that's why I'm doing this. For just this look that started the night after I buried my mother. In that kitchen in Bel Air. She gave me this same look and somehow, I'm growing...addicted to it. *Yesu.*

'My father was different. He never called it "artistic nonsense". He backed me. Even when it cost him. Especially when it cost him.' I pause. I should stop. Seriously. 'This isn't about the Biney name. It's about honouring the only man who ever believed in me.'

I look out at the sea, let the silence swallow the confession I'll never say out loud: that losing my father was the day my compass broke. But something about the way she's continuing to look at me now—like I'm more than my money or my sins—undoes me.

And that's when I give in.

I drag her to me.

And I kiss her.

Hard and merciless. It's the only language I still speak

well. It's won me awards, after all. And sometimes tried and true win wars.

'Hate me if you must,' I whisper, voice raw against her lips, 'but you've been driving me fucking crazy.'

Cilla

I freeze.

No, I *burn*.

My first instinct is to push him away, to remind him of everything this isn't. But my mouth doesn't listen. My body doesn't either. I'm kissing him back before I even realise it. Open-mouthed. Hot-headed. And sweet heaven, against my better judgement, open-hearted. The kind of kiss that makes your spine tingle and your mind blank.

God, I've missed this. Him.

His taste is familiar, warm and dark, tinged with longing and grief and regret. His hands slide to my waist, pulling me closer, and I let him. I shouldn't. I know I shouldn't. But I do.

Because I'm tired of fighting this. Of pretending that this isn't the most alive I've felt in weeks. *Months*, even.

His lips coax mine open and everything tilts.

For one long, dangerous moment, I forget the terms of our arrangement. I forget his sharp tongue and my sharper righteous truths. I forget the contract. The lie that doesn't feel like a lie any more. The family legacy pulsing in the foundation of all of this.

His hands are reverent and rough at once, fingers pressing into my hips, like he's grounding himself with my body. And mine? Mine are in his hair. Tangling. Gripping. Losing myself in something that's not fake at all.

Then too soon, but not soon enough, I remember.

I remember the morning after. The silence. The cold shut

out. The bruising distance he put between us after I dare to run, to protect myself from yet another Biney.

But even now, there's heat behind that distance. Still smouldering when I pull back just enough to breathe. Because it turns out, pulling back didn't equate to pulling *away*, so our foreheads remain touching. Our breaths still mingling.

'This doesn't mean anything,' I whisper, my voice trembling.

His eyes meet mine. Hungry. Haunted. 'Sure,' he mocks a little hoarsely, but there's the tiniest hesitation, the tiniest crack.

And I don't say it out loud, but I know it, even as I pretend I don't. Where this is headed? It's going to ruin me. But for good or ill, I'm not ready to stop. Not yet.

'We're still pretending,' I insist, my voice trembling.

His mouth curves in that devastating way that makes my stomach dip and heave. 'Then stop me. Now, Cilla, because if you don't I will take more.'

He waits. Watches. The ferocious predator waiting to pounce.

I don't. *Because I can't.*

He swoops back in and his kiss is a furnace, igniting everything I've worked so hard to keep cold. The wind tugs at my hair as his hands spread across my back, pulling me flush against the solid heat of his chest. Somewhere, the Mediterranean sighs against the yacht's hull. Somewhere, the sun slides low over the horizon. But here—here it's only us. And this fire we can't seem to douse.

My hands—traitorous things—slip beneath his linen shirt, tracing the ridges of his abs, the fine line of hair trailing downward. His body jerks, a hiss escaping between clenched teeth. He lifts me with maddening ease, setting me down on one of the wide cushioned lounges.

'Cilla,' he breathes, like it's a prayer and a curse all at once. 'I mean it. Tell me to stop.'

I look up at him, chest heaving, lips tingling, every cell in my body wired and wild. 'I still can,' I whisper. 'And maybe I will. At any time.'

But I still don't.

Because even now, even when his mouth finds the hollow of my throat, when his hands slide down my hips and back up beneath the thin fabric of my cover-up, I don't want to stop. I want to feel. To take. To burn again, just this once.

His name escapes my lips in a breathy plea as he coaxes reactions from my body with devastating precision. Fingers trailing up my thigh, down my spine. Mouth everywhere. Worshipping. Claiming. Undoing.

He drags his lips down the curve of my shoulder, then lower, until I'm arching off the cushions with a gasp. My fingers dig into his back. My toes curl into the soft throw beneath me. I've never been touched like this. Never felt so wanted. So consumed.

'This doesn't mean anything,' I lie again, trembling against him.

He growls something into my skin, something rough and primal, and his hands tighten on my hips. Then Ashon shuts me up, lies and all, the best way he knows how. By parting my thighs and feasting on me. Me plucking my pebbled nipples, him tonguing me and fingering me and tasting me until I see beyond skies into heaven.

I shatter with his name on my lips, my body shuddering as pleasure rips through me like a wave crashing on the shore.

For a moment, the world disappears. It's just sensation and heat and the throb of my pulse.

But then—

Then it crashes back.

My breath catches. Shame, sharp and bright, slices through the haze. What have I done?

I shove gently at his chest. He stills, blinking down at me like he's just surfaced from the same deep tide.

'No,' I whisper. 'We can't.'

His jaw flexes. 'We already did.'

'I can't do this. Not again.'

I scramble upright, tugging the edge of my kaftan back into place, heat rising in my cheeks for an entirely different reason now. I don't look at him. I can't. Because if I do, I'll lose every shred of control I just clawed back.

I move for the steps but his voice stops me.

Mocking. Low. Possessive.

'Running off again, I see. Remember, you won't get very far this time, wife. Not with my ring on your finger and my baby in your belly.'

I freeze.

Then keep walking, even though my legs feel like they'll give out at any moment.

Because the worst part isn't that he's right.

It's that I want to go back, beg for more. More than I want my next breath.

CHAPTER SEVEN

Ashon

WHAT THE HELL just happened?

I'm still standing there, shirt half-unbuttoned, her taste on my tongue, her heat clinging to my skin like a sexy ghost—and she's already gone. Slipped away like a wisp of smoke through my fingers.

Again.

I drag a hand over my jaw, my breath still ragged, my body pulsing with need and frustration and something far more dangerous.

Will I never learn?

I should be furious. Hell, I *am* furious. Not just with her for walking away again, for leaving me in this state like I'm some lovesick fool, but with myself. Because I let it happen. Because I *wanted* it to happen. Because for one goddamn minute, I let go of the plan, the performance, and I let myself feel.

I stalk across the deck, each step a barely restrained explosion. The teak floor groans under my weight. The horizon mocks me with its white-hot perfection, the air still humming with the echo of her moan, her hands, the soft tremble of her body under mine.

It wasn't enough. But it was too much.

I grip the railing, muscles tight and knuckles creaking.

The sea stretches out before me, dark and glittering like a cruel mirror.

And I force myself to see beyond the blazing lust and clawing need. To our conversation. To how she asked me earlier, how long this goes on for. When Nana would hold up his end of the bargain. Maybe it's a blessing this thing stopped when it did.

Because maybe that is all she cared about?

A fucking piece of land? Not the moment we shared at the clinic? Not the sound of our baby's heartbeat, echoing through the sterile room like a promise?

I draw the ultrasound picture from my pocket once more, falling effortlessly back into that moment.

It gutted me in a way I didn't expect.

Because an astonishing part of me wanted to hold onto it. Make it real.

Make us real.

The admission hits me square in the chest now, a truth clawing its way up.

I want my child.

This fragile, terrifying thing we've made together.

The need to protect it—to protect *them*—is carving something open inside me I didn't know I still had. Something raw. Human. Real.

But… God help me. I also want more of those moments. Power and legacy. Yes. But I'm the greedy bastard who also wants even more. Not what my grandfather believes is the culmination of every man's dream but what my father had with my mother.

I want a semblance of that with her.

I want it all. Not just the version I show the world. Not just the roles we agreed to play.

I want *Cilla.*

And what the hell am I supposed to do with that? I'm not built for tenderness. For vulnerability. I'm built for domination as I'm constantly reminded. For winning.

So I do what I've always done when my emotions threaten to drown me—

I dive.

I fold the image back into my pocket, shrug out of my shirt, strip to my briefs and launch myself over the edge of the yacht.

The water hits like fire and ice, stealing my breath. But it's a relief. It cuts through the heat in my veins, the ache in my body, the tangled mess in my chest.

I swim hard and fast, pushing against the current, trying to exorcise the ghost of her lips, her scent, the sound of her whispering *this doesn't mean anything.*

Because I know that's bullshit. Whether we wanted it to or not, it does.

It *does.*

And that's the goddamn problem.

Cilla

The chopper hums low over the Mediterranean as Cap Ferrat shrinks behind us, a glittering crescent of wealth and shadowed memory. Ashon sits beside me, legs splayed wide, one hand resting on the seat between us—close but not touching. We haven't spoken since take-off. Not much since that outing on the yacht and the clinch that shouldn't have happened if I'm honest.

A truce, yes. Comfortable? Not exactly.

He's in work mode now. Clean-shaven with sunglasses. Black button-down shirt sleeves rolled to the elbows and confidence tailored to his skin. Stupidly hot beyond measure or fairness. He's quiet but humming with the energy of someone about to dominate a room. The man the world calls a prodigy. The one I first noticed not in a boardroom or on a red carpet, but in a dim projection booth in LA, hunched over a monitor, coaxing colour into truth.

That's what I remember. Not the headlines or the glitz. But his quiet brilliance. That impossible focus.

We land at the converted vineyard thirty minutes later. It's a rustic-modern hub now, half-production studio, half artist colony—a test site for the Obibini studio model: empower through access, not pity. The idea is brilliant. The implementation? That's what Ashon's here for.

I trail behind him, my heels crunching the gravel, still unsure why I decided to tag along when he threw the offer at me like a king throwing bread to peasants. Maybe I'm a glutton for punishment. Maybe I want to see him in his true element once more, see if he passes some sort of test I'm not even aware of?

The staff part like petals for a sun they recognise. And he is dazzling, directing without ego, listening with intent, sketching ideas onto whiteboards, switching between English, French and Fante like they were coded into his DNA.

A few of them greet me too. Politely. With that odd, sideways curiosity reserved for political wives or reality TV stars. I smile and shake hands. Nod when expected.

But mostly I watch him.

Ashon Biney, my husband, is magnificent when he's in his element. There's no other word for it. He's not just powerful, he's purposeful. It's sexy in a way that makes my throat dry and my brain combust. He laughs once, a real one, and the sound ricochets through me like a memory. Like that night. The night we shouldn't have had and the one I haven't stopped thinking about.

I sit in a shaded corner with a notebook, pretending to jot observations. Really, I'm just trying not to melt.

This is dangerous. Not just because of what's between us physically, but because—against all logic—I'm fearing that I'm starting to *like* him. That hearing him speak of his father last night and this morning has given me another glimpse into the man behind the myth and that man…

Yes, he's relentless, but not just for power's sake. He's chasing something lasting. I see it now. In the way he talks about legacy. In the reverence when he speaks of his father's belief in him. He's trying to build something that outlives the fame, the gloss, the noise. And isn't that what I'm trying to do, in my own way? Especially now that I'm carrying a future neither of us expected?

Worse, I don't need to do more than simply close my eyes to picture him cradling our child. Fierce and flawed and terrifyingly tender. I can almost feel what it would be like to trust him with more than my body.

God help me, do I already more than like him?

Because that's a problem. A big one.

Because I swore I'd come into this with clear eyes. A plan. I'd get the land, restore my mother's dignity and my father's memory, and then walk away with my head held high.

But what happens if I want…if I want a different deal that I've made for myself? What if I want…more. I've spent years sharpening that goal like a blade—getting back what the Bineys stole. It consumed me after I lost my father. Gave me purpose even when I had no money or power. Just pain and a promise to do right by the parents who gave me everything they could. And now…now the plan is blurring at the edges.

Because I'm not just their daughter any more.

I'm a mother. And a wife.

Even if it's just for show, the reality of it all has started to press against my heart. I don't just want justice. I want peace when all of this is done. A future where I don't have to fight every single day to prove my worth or my claim. Where my child won't grow up carrying the bitterness I've worn like armour for so long.

And the most terrifying part? I wonder what Ashon would say if he knew that.

If he'd still see me as the principled woman who stood in his study demanding fairness…or just another person rewriting the script halfway through.

Dear God, we've been married less than a fortnight and I'm already crumbling?

Questions and impossible desires haunt me as we leave the production and head for the helipad.

When we're back in the air—closer now, the helicopter a tin can of tension—I finally break the silence. Mostly because I can't stand my own thoughts. 'That went well.'

Ashon hums, his eyes on his phone. 'It's a strong pilot. Might even syndicate and expand sooner than expected.'

'You're building something remarkable,' I say, my voice softer than I intend. 'It's…it's different from what people expect of you.'

He lifts his head at that. Tilts it slightly, assessing. 'And what *do* people expect of me, Cilla?'

I shrug. 'Headlines. Drama. Power plays. This feels more… subtle. Emotion that creeps up on you.'

Something glints in his eyes. 'And you? What do you expect of me?'

His tone is unreadable, but it coils around me anyway. I should say something light. Dismissive. But my recent thoughts crowd every corner of my brain. 'Do you really want to know?'

His gaze sharpens. 'I wouldn't ask if I didn't. I'm sure you know that about me.'

'Do I? I think you care more than you want people to see, which makes me wonder if…'

'If?' he probes. I feel every ounce of his focus drilling into me.

'If your still waters run deeper than the legacy you pursue so doggedly?'

I realise what I'm really asking. And I hold my breath, caught between wanting to see beneath the surface and hoping he doesn't answer because I'm mildly terrified of what either would imply. For me. For this excavation of feelings I'm not sure I want to unearth.

He's silent. Then, abruptly, he shakes his head. 'Careful. You keep digging and I might mistake you for a journalist. Or worse, one of those paparazzo,' he drawls but I catch the lingering probing of my face.

The face I turn away to look out the window because his dig lands harder than it should and I frantically hide the sting. 'I'm not here to write a story, Ashon. I'm here because we made a deal.' And, oh yes, the reminder is as much for him as for me.

His fingers tap idly on his thigh. 'Right. The land. The legacy. The baby.'

There's something in his voice, sharp and clipped.

'Why do you say it like that?'

'Like what?'

'Like it's all just…business.'

His jaw flexes. 'Isn't it what you're at pains to remind me at every turn?'

My mouth goes dry. The helicopter dips slightly in altitude, the sun cutting a halo around his remote profile.

We land and he walks me, courteous as ever, into the villa.

'I need to touch base with Renée and with Theo about the blueprints for the studio. I might be a while. I'll have dinner organised for you. Goodnight, Cilla,' he says.

And just like that, before I can snap that I can organise my own dinner, thanks, he's gone.

And in the silence, I listen to my heart, just like the thoughts I dared to entertain, lurching into spaces it shouldn't.

Surprise, surprise, I don't sleep. And yes, I'm fully aware it's probably my own fault.

It'd be easy to blame it on pregnancy and the almost non-existent morning sickness. But I can't stoop to that level of disingenuousness. My hand glides over my belly, which is beginning to harden just a little bit, but I don't…can't think about my baby.

Not when my mind is consumed by Ashon.

I don't know what hurts more, his distance or my longing.

The villa is quiet, too quiet, the kind of stillness that amplifies your thoughts until they're too loud to ignore. I've already tried reading. Pacing.

Even a bath with the fancy salts Renée packed. Nothing works. My body hums with unshed tension, but it's not just that. I'm haunted by the feel of Ashon's hands, the sound of his voice when he lets the mask slip. I'm haunted by possibilities and hidden desires that feel a little less hidden with each passing moment.

A little fed up with my insomnia and a lot fed up with myself, I sit up. Pad barefoot to the small writing desk by the window. After a moment's hesitation, I pull open the journal I've kept since that morning after. I'm not even sure why I picked up the teenage habit I abandoned a long time ago, but I'm not ashamed to say it helped through those first days.

I flip through pages of observations, lies I've told myself, dreams I've buried, grievances I've inked and circled like my own personal dartboard.

Then, without fully thinking, I flip to a fresh page and I write: *What if I'm not pretending any more?*

The stark, heart-pounding words terrify me enough that I snap the book shut, rush across the room, towards the bed as if it wasn't the lonely sanctuary I fled from minutes ago.

But the thought of more tossing and turning makes me veer away from it. I hate that I half-wish Ashon is lingering in the hallways.

But he's not.

Only moonlight and silence greets me, the floors cool beneath my bare feet. I wander and eventually, I find myself in the cinema room.

It's luxurious, of course, like everything else in this spectacular place—velvet recliners, surround sound, a screen that could rival any theatre.

I stop long enough to snag a small box of sweets, then sink into a seat, remote in hand, and start flicking through channels like I don't have a motive.

But I do. One that's been teasing the back of my mind since this afternoon.

Ten minutes in, I've given up the charade.

Ashon's second film, *Fracture Point*, plays on the screen fast-forwarded to the fifty-fifth minute. It's a quiet scene, one of my favourites. His character sitting alone on a rooftop, talking about fathers and failure. It's raw, magnetic. He's barely acting. Even then, he was carrying the weight of legacy.

'I always wondered if that rooftop monologue was scripted,' I murmur aloud.

A voice answers from the dark. 'It wasn't.'

I start and several pieces of wine gums go flying. The same way my heartbeat is.

Spinning around, I see Ashon leaning against the doorway, arms folded, wearing only low-slung lounge pants and a sardonic smile. 'I wondered how long it would take for you to cave and watch me.'

'I wasn't watching you,' I lie because I'm weak but not stupid. 'I'm watching something you made.'

He steps into the room and the light from the screen bathes his masculine beauty. 'Same difference, wife. So what, then? Academic curiosity? Artistic appreciation?' he drawls, eyes gleaming.

My fingers tighten around the remote and I summon my most haughty expression. 'I was channel surfing.'

He laughs, low and disbelieving. 'Sure you were.'

I don't move as he approaches, don't even pretend to look away. I'm not sure I could. 'It's a good movie. Your actor is exceptional in it.'

'I know.' He stops in front of me, blocking out the heartthrob on the screen. For a wild moment, I wonder if that's why he's positioned himself this way. My senses leap far too wildly at that thought. 'But that's not why you're watching it tonight, is it?'

I don't answer. The way my instinct is flailing tells me I don't need to. Ashon Biney is clever. Wildly intuitive. And I sense that scrambling for other excuses will only dig my hole deeper.

His hand cups my jaw, thumb brushing the corner of my mouth. My skin tightens in anticipation. My breath snags.

'You keep finding new ways to haunt me,' he murmurs, half-contemplative, half-disgruntled. Wholly fascinating in its exposition. 'In quite unique and unexpected ways.'

'And? Are you going to pretend you don't like it?'

'No, my sweet wife, I like to leave the pretence on the

screen.' A tight smile twitched at the corner of his mouth. 'And for my grandfather.'

'So what are you saying? That this…' I make a vague gesture at the hand holding me captive, 'Is something that intrigues you?'

'Oh yes, enough to drive me from my bed. Enough to want to dig deeper, discover why you have this…' He pauses and his jaw ripples with tension.

'Go on, say it. Don't be shy.'

Again a smile that is crashed out by intense speculation long before it reaches his eyes. 'Do you know how many I've told about my father? About this place and what it means?'

I open my mouth but the words dry up when his gaze drops to it, his eyes igniting into a blaze.

'Very, very few. And those people I trust.'

I fight the hurt tightening like a vice around my chest. 'And you don't trust me.'

'When we keep circling each other like gladiators in a blood-stained arena?' His voice is rough-edged with something compulsive. And that introspection deepens until I want to squirm. 'Most would think me a fool if I did.'

'I don't care about other people,' I blurt before I can stop myself. 'What do you think?'

He stiffens, then his nostrils flare. 'Like I said, I'm in no hurry to race to the credits.'

'Or you're hedging, waiting for the hammer to fall?'

'Do you blame me?'

'Yes, I do. You might want to blame others for letting you down but shutting yourself off is a choice you made. So—'

'Let's find other uses for this sharp tongue, I think, wife,' he cuts through me, then follows with a sound, half-growl, all animal, leaps from his throat.

I know what's coming long before he lowers his head.

The remote leaves my bruising grip a nanosecond before our mouths crash together, urgent and unapologetic.

His hands find my waist, pulling me into his lap as I straddle him in the recliner. I'm not wearing much, just my thong and one of the long nighties that formed my trousseau—the hem of which is shoved up to enable my thighs to frame his.

The feel of his bare chest beneath my palms makes my head spin.

We kiss like we're starving. Like the walls we've built are paper-thin tonight.

His lips trail down my neck, my collarbone, until he's got me gasping. I grind against him, chasing something I shouldn't want this badly. He groans, hard and low as I rock on his steel-hard erection, moaning at the memories reeling through my brain and dying with the need to relive them.

After an age, Ashon shifts, sliding down, fingers hooking in my underwear. That primal, determined look, the one he wore on the yacht, is back in his face and I know he's seconds away from calculating my downfall. From taking me apart with his magic hands and lips and teeth.

But no, not tonight. I falter a little when his fingers graze my clit, then suck in a composing breath and stop him. 'Maybe it makes you feel manly to think you need to blow my mind all the time,' I say, panting. 'But I have something to give too.'

He goes still. Then slowly, he leans back into the armchair, eyes burning.

'Oh yeah? Show me what you've got then.' His voice is rough. A dare.

Nerves pinch me, a voice rumbling at the back of my mind with the need to know what the hell I'm thinking.

But I push it away, lower myself between his thighs, until my knees meet the plush carpet.

Sliding my hands into his waistband, I pause, raise an eyebrow.

He holds out for one second, two.

Then with a flash of curious vulnerability and a touch of helplessness that punches something into my chest, Ashon lifts up, his six-pack clenching so deliciously in the flickering light my mouth waters.

And I pull his loungers down.

His cock springs free and I can't help it. I gasp. At his beauty. His girth. In fresh recollection of what delights this shaft brought me.

And because I'm at risk of tumbling back down that dangerous rabbit hole, I slide my hands up his taut thighs, lean in closer, let my mouth move with purpose.

He groans my name at the first taste, his fingers tangling in my hair, and for a moment, I feel powerful. Worshipped. Necessary.

I seize the moment, take control and work this man who so effortlessly consumes my hours and my life, into a frothing frenzy. I lick and suck and tease until grunts and groans turn to guttural pleas and spicy curses. Where a promise is tossed here and a hot, sexy threat is snarled at me.

And all through it I smile, meet eyes turned black fire and offer him my throat.

He hisses, tightens his grip. 'You…you're a damn sorceress, you know that?' he slurs.

'And do you want this sorceress to stop. Or do you want to finish?'

'You know damn well, what I want, wife,' he rasps.

Something about the label fills me with a combination of higher power and despair. I push the latter away, embrace the former. I swirl my tongue around his bulbous crown. 'Then do it. Your turn to show me what you got…husband.'

He thickens between my lips, then with a rumbling roar no less spectacular for its muted ferocity, Ashon climaxes. And dear heaven but I can't help but stare, consume every moment of his pleasure, store it deep down, for what purpose I'm too chicken to examine right now.

And when it's over—when he's breathless and glassy-eyed—he pulls me into his lap again, cradles my face like I'm more than just a beautiful distraction. And that's when the panic sets in.

Because this is starting to feel like something real.

And I don't know how to stop it.

Leave, then. Do the necessary. Protect yourself.

Aware he's watching my every move, I rise. But before I can retreat, he catches my wrist.

'Not this time,' he says, eyes gleaming with something too complex, too potent, to name.

And then he kisses me.

Not hard but slow, sure, devastating, like he's imprinting something he won't say aloud. My breath stutters, caught between the soft glide of his mouth and the sudden, terrifying warmth blooming in my chest.

Before I can think, before I can stop him, he sweeps me into his arms.

'Ashon—'

'Relax,' he rasps, his voice rough with something dangerously close to tenderness. A mellowing I might be enjoying a little too much. 'You're right, I'm a firm believer in the concept of *quid pro quo* so the least I can do is help you back to your bed. Besides, I'm discovering finding my pregnant wife literally barefoot and walking through my house is digging up all sorts of primal urges I won't bore you with so the quicker I get you to your bed, the better for both of us, hmm?'

I want to argue, but I don't. Because I don't want to leave him just yet. Not really.

He carries me down the corridor, the light from the cinema flickering behind us. When my head lulls to rest against his chest I allow it, letting the steady beat of his heart echo the chaos and yearning in mine.

At my bedroom door, he pauses, looks down at me. 'I'm looking forward to Botswana.'

My breath hitches. 'Why?'

There's a flicker in his eyes. Calculation. Anticipation. Something deeper, indecipherable. 'Because I suspect,' he murmurs as the walks into my bedroom and lowers me to the bed, 'there's another plot twist coming in our particular script.'

He brushes my cheek with his thumb. One last kiss, potent and lingering. And then he steps back looking much too composed much too soon while leaving me reeling.

'Goodnight, Cilla,' he says in that deep voice.

I probably respond or I don't. But I welcome the drowsiness that arrives quickly, as if now the stimulus of Ashon has been delivered, my body is ready for rest.

And as I shut my eyes, and sigh into my pillow, my heart a confused, fluttering mess, his words echo in my head.

Plot twist. Plot twist. Plot twist.

I'm not sure whether I want it.

But I'm starting to think my heart and mind will decide it for me, with or without my permission.

Ashon

The jet hums like a soundtrack I can't fall asleep to, cabin lights dimmed to a dusky gold. Outside, the sky is ink-black, the stars swallowed by altitude.

Cilla sleeps in the private bedroom, one pale sheet thrown over her body, one steady rise of breath, and everything in me aching to be next to her. Spooned behind her, palm curved over the small swell of her belly, feeling what's mine...*ours*... shift between us like a living connection.

Instead I'm out here, wide-awake and restless, replaying every frame of last night like I'm directing it again in my head: the scrape of her nails, the rasp of her voice, the power in the way she took me apart and then *tried* once again to slip away. The look in her eyes as she did it all—equal parts defiance, apprehension and determination—won't leave me alone.

For one reckless heartbeat I'd toyed with what could've been if she'd wanted *me* for me, not land or leverage. Like I was simply a man—*her* man. The one who could boldly answer that yes, I could trust and yes, I could expose my feelings and yes, I could say to hell with past histories and lessons learned about chancers and gold diggers. That I could harness a fraction of the certainty my father held when he looked at me with hope and told me *family is everything.* Except I was right there, bearing witness to the truth that family wasn't everything to everyone. That self-worth was measured by accolades and power.

But... God help me, I must be a fool because I want that look again, *make believe or not.* I want it regardless of the cost and consequence. And what does that make me if not the fool I was that night in LA?

I don't care about what other people think...

I rub a hand over my jaw, knuckles tight. My father used to say altitude makes the truth louder. Right now it's deafening.

Seriously? You're catching feelings for your fake wife?

I want to growl *so what*? But even the silent words stay locked in my chest, a step too bold and brazen and incredibly stupid to be given room to grow.

The phone buzzes. Renée. With more than a chest full of relieved gratitude, I answer the call.

'Yes?'

A pause. 'Catch you at a bad time?'

I glance at towards the bedroom, grit my teeth. 'Not at all.'

'Okay…how's the honeymoon going?'

Great in parts. Frustration in most. Infernal longing I can't rid myself of. 'You've never expressed interest in my personal relationships. Let's not change what works, hmm?'

'I could argue that you've never put a ring on any of the others, but okay. I'll stick to business,' she returns.

'Thanks,' I growl.

I hear the smirk in her voice before she clears it. 'Projects are sailing,' she reports. 'Botswana team's prepped for your visit, Italian site is back on schedule.' She continues with a brisk report of every project, taking my mind off the woman occupying it all of twenty minutes before she's done.

'Enjoy the honeymoon—if you remember you're on one.'

I grunt.

She stays on a beat. 'You all right, Ash?'

Not even close.

'Fine,' I lie. She hears it but lets it go.

I've barely pocketed the phone when it rings again—my lead attorney.

'I have good news. The final deed transfers are ready. By dawn you'll own the site outright and well on your way to realising your dreams, Mr Biney.'

Years of fighting for my legacy and the finish line is hours away. I should feel triumphant.

Instead a cold weight settles in my chest because the moment the ink dries, the marriage-of-convenience loses its only stated purpose.

Doesn't it?

Will she even stay the year we agreed or will she insist on immediately dissolving this union regardless that she's carrying my child.

I close my eyes, head thumping against the leather seat. The plan was simple: get the land, build the studio, become the Biney who finally lived up to the name.

She gets her family's property back, I get my father's dream secured.

We part ways amicably.

Except nothing feels simple any more.

Images carousel through my mind. Cilla's shy hand sliding over the ultrasound photo. Her laughing with a fisherman's wife on the Cap Ferrat pier. The way she said *'I think he'd be proud of you.'* No one has ever spoken my father's memory back to me so gently.

It was a balm and a blade.

I'm used to fighting for things. Winning them. But keeping something—*someone*—requires a different muscle, one I'm not sure I ever exercised. I thrive in power and empire-building and tailoring a narrative to achieve my epic ends, not indulging in feelings of the non-carnal kinds. Love is a language I only know how to invoke others to speak on film. Hell, I never even realised how much I needed my father's until I had to live without it. And the memory of that loss, that emptiness, is a searing reminder not to toy with invoking even the ghost of it. Besides, what do I have to offer except what I've already given her, wealth and my name…for a time?

What if I offer her more and she laughs? What if she says yes and I fail her the way Nana always said I'd fail everything?

Cilla shifts in the bed, just a sigh and a tumble of braids across the pillow. The sheet dips low on her hip. Moonlight paints her skin silver. She looks fragile. She looks unstoppable. She looks like temptation and *mine*, and the realisation slices clean through my defenses.

Maybe the true plot twist isn't locking down the deed and my legacy.

Maybe it's standing in front of Cilla—and the world—taking complete possession of all that truly matters and saying this marriage isn't ending.

That the child she carries won't grow up watching his parents pretend.

That the studio, the land, the legacy will carry both our names. If she wants it to?

But to do that, I have to risk the one thing I've guarded harder than the inheritance, this emotional fortress I've built.

My father's voice echoes—*You'll see.* Maybe this is what he meant.

I scrub both hands over my face, then stand. The cabin is still, only the soft click of the bedroom door latch breaks the quiet as I open it.

I don't wake her, just watch her breathe, memorise the calm before we step into whatever storm Botswana brings.

Land or legacy or life or…*even more.* For the first time, I don't know which I want more, which I'd want to choose.

Some plot twists you don't write, they write themselves and rewrite you.

And maybe, when the sun rises over the Okavango, I'll decide what I'm prepared to do to give this story a different ending.

If at all.

CHAPTER EIGHT

Cilla

BOTSWANA GREETS US like a promise wrapped in heat and gold.

The Biney jet touches down on a private strip carved between jackal-berry trees and tall, whispering grasses.

A welcome delegation waits—a quartet of dancers in beaded skirts, a brass band, a photographer who can't decide whether to aim at Ashon or at me.

Ashon helps me down the mobile stairs. His hand lingers at my waist, steady and sure. There's something new in his eyes—resolve, almost fierce. He's watching me the way he studies a movie set right before he shouts 'Action'. With intent and hunger, ready to rewrite the scene if it doesn't serve the story.

'Expecting another red carpet?' I tease, adjusting my sunhat.

'Just making sure you don't run,' he murmurs, even-toned but with that watchful determination very much present. 'Botswana's a long sprint home, wife.'

'Try me. I've been upping my cardio.'

He laughs, that low warm sound that always skims my skin like velvet. We climb into an air-conditioned safari vehicle lined in creamy leather. Champagne appears but is waved away by Ashon before I can refuse and I gratefully accept the chilled mineral water he passes me.

A guide launches into delighted facts about elephants and delta floods. But my attention keeps hooking on Ashon's profile—the relaxed line of his shoulders at odds with the hard curve of a smile he doesn't quite hide.

Cap Ferrat feels miles away, but not forgotten, if that heat lurking in his brown eyes is an indication.

My own heat is stirring when the resort finally rises ahead, stilted villas draped in thatch, private plunge pools catching late afternoon sun. Ashon leans close, lips brushing my ear. 'I'm assured they have a cinema room.'

My pulse flares. 'And you plan a rerun, do you, or a brand-new screening?' I ask, a pulse for that daring and power from last night, stealing through my blood.

'That depends entirely on which seat you take,' he counters, wicked.

I swallow a laugh and the lump of anticipation and deep, deep longing behind it.

And because that frightens the hell out of me, the second we're shown into our accommodation I claim jetlag as an excuse to flee to my allocated bedroom.

Very much aware Ashon's eyes follow me like a tether on a very short leash.

I wake three hours later in gauzy twilight, tangled in linen sheets and a dream so vivid I can still taste him. The movie-dark room, his hands in my hair, my desperate moan swallowed by his kiss. My body remembers every pulse of it, humming like a struck chord.

A knock sounds, then the door opens at my husky response.

The man I've just been dreaming about enters with a silver tray, his eyes immediately locking on me. He's ditched the linen suit for a charcoal T-shirt and soft slacks that cling where memory says my palms belong.

When I manage to drag my gaze away, I see what's on the tray. Ginger tea, grilled tilapia, papaya slices. As if my body lives to please him and betray me, my belly growls in mouthwatering response.

'You didn't eat on the plane. Couldn't risk you fainting again,' he says, voice gentle but implacable. 'Tea first. Then you can yell at me for waking you.'

I sit up, hair a mess, heart wilder than the delta beyond the deck. 'No yelling,' I manage, sucking in a deep breath. 'I was just…'

'Dreaming interesting dreams?' His brow lifts, like he already knows.

Heat rushes up my neck but I don't answer. In silence, he cuts up the fish and I let him feed me bites, followed by the juicy papaya.

When I reach for the cup, my fingers brush his instead. Electric, inevitable. I don't pull away.

His gaze drops to our hands, then climbs slowly to my mouth. He raises the cup himself and I take a sip. Then… as he lowers it, something inside me gives, the last flimsy barricade.

I release the cup and I tug. At him. At something that my body screams harder for.

He comes, the look in his eyes saying he's known this was as inevitable as I've feared.

The tray clinks onto the bedside table—forgotten—and suddenly his weight is sinking into the mattress, his lips finding mine, soft but unyielding.

The kiss starts careful, but caution burns faster than a blaze on the savannah.

His tongue teases mine and the taste of sweet ginger flickers between us. His palm skims under the loose sleep shirt I'd thrown on, finding skin, finding the new curve at my waist that shelters our child.

He pauses there, thumb stroking once, reverent. My breath hitches at the tenderness of it.

'You keep daring me,' he whispers against my throat. 'Dare me not to want every single part of you.'

'Do you?' I challenge.

He smiles. That arrogant, intensely smug and partly sardonic look. 'You need me to convince you, again?' he mutters.

My reply is a sigh that melts into a yes.

A fierce blaze consumes his expression, then he cups my face, kisses me again, longer, deeper, then trails open-mouthed caresses down the column of my neck.

Each one is a question. Can you deny this? Does this feel false to you?

And each time my hands, mouth and legs answer, wrapping around him, tasting him in return, fisting in his shirt, tugging. When he lifts it over his head, I rake hungry eyes over the chiselled planes of his chest.

In Cap Ferrat I worshipped him, now I want him imprinting every inch of me.

Clothing becomes an inconvenience, peeled away in breathless pauses. No rush, yet everything urgent. The air smells of hibiscus carried on the evening breeze, of sandalwood from his skin. He settles me back onto pillows, mouths the swell of my breast with aching slowness until I arch, and the dream is reality. Several flicks of his tongue then a tortuous suckle erupt moans that blend into the sultry air.

'Cilla,' he murmurs, voice low and raw. 'Now's the time to tell me to stop if—'

'Don't,' I whisper—plea, command, confession. 'Please, don't.'

He moves between my thighs, his eyes still locked on me as if I'm the only thing he wants to see, to experience. That's the thing about this man, his unwavering focus to the thing he desires.

Knowing…in this moment…that thing is me?

My breath shudders as he grips his large girth, poses it at my entrance. And he looks at me. Desire is very much present, intensely so. But there's that calculation too. That resolve that says every move, every act from here on out will bear great significance.

But I want him too much to parse through what's happening now, to catalogue later consequences. Or maybe I've already fallen, been conquered by them.

So I reach for him.

And he comes to me.

He slides inside with a thick groan that vibrates through my bones. 'Fuck. Cilla.'

I feel full, perfect, as though my body was waiting only for this. For him.

Eerily in tune, he stills, his grip tightening on my hips, one hand catching my chin with the kind of possessive reverence that makes me forget how to breathe. His eyes bore into mine, dark and unrelenting. 'Why do you make me feel like this?' he demands, voice low and jagged, as if the words cost him.

My breath trembles. 'Like what?'

His jaw clenches, the muscle ticking. 'Like losing control would be worth it. Like I'd burn down my empire just to keep you looking at me like that.'

I flinch because I know he means it. And because I want to believe it. But I can't afford to.

'Maybe you're just drunk on the power,' I say, tilting my

chin even as my voice shakes. 'You like the idea of owning the one woman who dared to walk away.'

His eyes flash, hard with something raw. 'Don't flatter yourself. This was never about ownership.'

'No?' I whisper. 'Then what is it?'

He leans in, voice a whisper against my lips. 'It's the way you challenge me. The way you never make it easy. And the way, God help me, you fit against me like you were carved to.'

The words hit somewhere deep, somewhere I've tried so hard to bury.

I want to tell him he terrifies me. That this—whatever this is—is starting to mean too much. But I can't.

Because if I speak, I might never be able to take it back.

So instead, I kiss him like a coward and a seductress, slow and fierce, because it's safer than the truth.

And neither of us says the thing we both came dangerously close to whispering into the silence.

We move together in languid waves in a slow claiming that feels dangerously close to the kind of emotional connection that should terrify.

Probably does terrify.

But the undiluted pleasure thickening my blood and fogging my brain allows no room for fear, as he thrusts and I scream for more.

And as we hurtle towards that sublime peak, I watch his face change—arrogance stripped, every emotion vivid in the dark: awe, hunger, something that looks like plans solidifying. Maybe even *hope*?

The sight part fractures my defenses because dreams want to become reality.

My hips rise, matching his rhythm, chasing heat that coils deeper each time he thrusts. He braces one hand above my head, the other clasping our entwined fingers beside my pillow, anchoring us.

Pleasure builds, a tide pulling me under. When it crests, I cry out his name, unguarded, and feel him shudder, spill, bury his face at my shoulder.

Silence after is half-taut, half-tender, humming with shared heartbeat. He slips from my body but not my embrace, rolling so I lie half-atop him, cheek on his chest. The evening wraps us warm, the rustle of reeds outside the only witness.

I could speak about fear, about the emotions clawing at the edges of my resolve, but words feel fragile, far too exposing and explosive. Instead, I trace idle circles over his heart.

He catches my hand, presses a kiss to my palm, and in the hush I think I hear him whisper, almost too softly, arrogantly, 'This plot twist I saw coming from far away.'

I close my eyes, undecided whether to laugh or cry, and drift in the sweet aftermath. Knowing dawn will bring its own iteration, but tonight we've written this scene together, one that doesn't include fleeing because I sense this time I won't get very far.

And for the first time I'm not even sure I want to run.

Ashon

She reaches for me barely an hour after we've collapsed in a tangle of sheets and sighs. Fingertips skim my ribs, slow and searching, then slip lower to cup the back of my thigh and pull. Between my legs to grip and caress. A silent invitation.

I'm weak and oh so damn ready enough to need no second one.

Maybe the pregnancy plays its part—some article I devoured once I heard I was to be a father, about hormones and heightened desire—but it's too soon for that, surely?

Whatever. The truth is, I want my temptress whether there's science behind it or not. And who am I to refuse my wife when she threads her leg over my hip and whispers my name like it's the only word she knows.

I fall on her, already savage and ravenous.

We kiss, mouths still swollen, still tasting of the papaya I fed her earlier. Her nails rake lightly along my shoulder blades. The sound she makes when our bodies fit again is a soft, desperate hum that undoes me. Recalibrates new goals I'm more eager than ever to pursue.

I hold her hips, guiding the slow press of heat and friction until her breath catches. Until my own control frays and we're moving together in an unhurried rhythm.

She clings to me, lips brushing my jaw, shuddering as release finds her first—quiet, but intense enough to arch her spine and drag me right after. We stay locked that way, every muscle trembling, until the wave ebbs and we return to the softness of the mattress and each other's skin.

Cilla drifts back to sleep almost on a sigh, lashes damp, mouth parted. I watch her breathe with my fingertips idle on the curve of her waist. Somewhere outside, night creatures sing and the delta air smells of rain building on the horizon.

I should let the contentment carry me under with her, but my mind spins.

We've spent a week in Cap Ferrat and haven't killed each other. Yet. Her laugh was bright and unguarded. Evidence, maybe, of a foundation I never expected.

Hell, we enjoyed pockets of harmony, which worked on and expanded could sustain…something. Isn't that what marriage is expounded to be about? Heady highs to be celebrated and inevitable lows which, if successfully battled through, makes it all worth it?

A pang of guilt pricks under my ribs. Highs and lows out

in the open are all well and good, but… I'm not even sure why I haven't told her yet about the deeds. Nana's lawyers will have probably finalised them by now.

It's the last box to tick, the final victory and I'm hiding from my inbox and keeping it from Cilla.

It isn't a lie, exactly, just timing. I convince myself she deserves this honeymoon unburdened. I push the guilt aside, stroke her hair off her forehead and breathe her in.

She stirs, dark hazel eyes blinking open. 'You're awake,' she murmurs, voice husky.

'Couldn't sleep. Was busy admiring my wife,' I say, letting my knuckles trace her arm. 'Come scouting with me tomorrow? There's a river village our Botswana team wants me to see.'

A flicker of disappointment darkens her gaze but she masks it fast. 'So this isn't just a honeymoon, it's a work trip for you too?' she asks, trying for lightness and nearly succeeding.

My first impulse is a sharp retort—*Legacy-building doesn't sleep, Cilla, and neither do I*—but I bite it back and force the tightness in my chest to ease.

'It's one meeting,' I say instead, brushing my thumb over her cheek. 'An hour to keep the dream alive, then the rest of the day is ours—canoes, elephants and whatever wildlife decides to photobomb us.'

She arches a brow. 'You're saying you won't answer emails from the boat?'

'I promise to ignore every buzzing device until the hippos start judging me.'

Her smile returns, slow and genuine, and the air between us lightens, warms something deep in my chest. I stroke a braid behind her ear and add, 'Tomorrow I'm your tour guide first, studio mogul second. Hold me to it.' Why is my breath imprisoned in my chest, waiting for her to do just that when I'm my own man?

She gives a small, satisfied nod and snuggles closer, the potential for barbs diffused—for tonight, at least—by the warmth curling around us both.

I settle her against me, feeling awe ripple through the guilt and ambition. Maybe the plot twist isn't manipulating a performance or gaining the upper hand with sex and seduction. Maybe it's lavishing her with the care I never saw modelled for long enough, building a family I didn't know I yearned for until I placed my hand on her belly and everything in me refused to let go.

For the first time, I'm not thinking about land or legacy. I'm thinking about tomorrow. Her laughter echoing across the delta, our child growing in her belly and how to keep this feeling long after the ink is dry.

Cilla

We glide upriver in a flat-bottom skiff, papyrus brushing the hull, sunlight fractured into gold shards across the water. Hippos grunt somewhere downstream and a heron lifts off on slow, deliberate wingbeats. Ashon stands at the bow beside the local fixer named Mpho, a quick-smiling woman in khaki, and an assistant director flown in from Jo'burg, a lanky guy named Nico who fidgets with his camera like it's an extra limb.

Ashon turns, and the shiver over my skin tells me he's looking at me even though his eyes are covered by designer shades.

'What do you think?' He doesn't need to shout, his deep voice carries over the engine's soft whine. 'Could you picture a colonial-era trading post here? Opening sequence, 1880s—dusty dock, smugglers, forbidden cargo?'

I move to his side, bracing a palm on the rail. Nope, I'm not going to acknowledge the way my heart leapt. Not at his question, but at the fact that he's seeking my opinion.

I look around for a moment, the thrill of past projects and future possibilities making my pulse gallop. 'You'll need period boats, but the backdrop's perfect. Those fig trees could swallow a set whole.' I point to a spot of higher ground. 'Raise your façade there—wide-angle sweep, sun at your actors' backs. Instant cinematic nostalgia.'

He whistles low, pleased, then a flash of that devastating smile. 'You sure you're on sabbatical? Because I could use a location producer who sees light like that.'

Just like that? My breath catches. I yearn to yank off his shades, look into his eyes and verify he's not toying with me and my emotions.

Behind his shoulder Nico's head snaps up, interest sparking in eyes that linger on me a beat longer than polite. 'You work in film?'

'Documentaries,' I reply, summoning a smile despite being a little disgruntled at the interruption. And the knowledge that Ashon's watching me too, perhaps gauging my reaction to his maybe not-too-careless reply. 'Story rescue missions, mostly dealing with natural disasters.'

Nico replies with something I don't hear because all I can see is Ashon prowling towards me. He clears his throat—subtle but unmistakable—and drapes an arm across my shoulders when he reaches me. 'I should really punish you,' he murmurs in my ear, even with an edge.

My eyes widen. 'Punish me? For what?'

'For wasting auteur DNA on turndown service,' he grates,

then to Nico, 'She's understating her accomplishments. Her last doc took home a Tribeca audience award.'

I tell myself I mistake the punch of pride in his voice, conflating it with the thrill of being punished…in the bedroom… by my husband. Where I make him quake with the force of my allure.

I want more of that. Extensively. For ever?

Ashon's eyes narrow on me. 'What is lurking in that clever mind?'

'Plot twists,' I murmur before I can stop myself.

He stiffens but his eyes *ignite*. 'Which kind?'

'The kinds I shouldn't entertain beyond the parameters of what we agreed.'

'But you are?' he presses, almost urgently, his eyes now burning.

I purse my lips, terrified I've already left my flanks wide open.

'Would it help to know I too have considered…things?'

My eyes widen. 'Really? You—'

Beside us Nico grunts. 'Impressive.'

Ashon's arm tightens, proprietary, just as disgruntled at the interruption. I feel a flicker of heat that has nothing to do with the Botswana sun. Then his body moves, planting himself firmly between me and Nico. It would be funny if it didn't evoke distinctly *un*-feminist feelings inside me.

We drift to a stop near a sandy bank and his mouth drifts over my temple. 'To be revisited?'

I give a jerky nod as Mpho kills the engine and hops out to test the footing, then waves us onshore. The instant my sandals hit the warm ochre sand, Ashon launches into pitch mode. Bigger, louder, gesturing like a conductor directing an invisible orchestra. Passion and power and utterly unapologetic about either.

'A three-generation feud—trade empire versus missionary outfit, enemies turned reluctant partners, then lovers. Legacy poisoned by greed. Present-day descendants forced to uncover buried sins.'

'Generational enemies-to-lovers,' I muse, heartbeat quickening. 'Epic. Messy. People will eat it up.'

He nods, one corner of his sinfully sensual lips quirking. 'You approve?'

'Hmm. I'd watch it twice.'

His eyes gleam and I know he's thinking back to heated acts in cinema rooms. 'Good, because I want you advising on the historical beat sheet.'

Nico coughs, a polite bid to re-enter the conversation, and asks a technical question about natural light reflectors. Ashon answers, but the guy's gaze keeps flicking to my bare legs peeking from my wrap skirt. I'm more amused than flattered. Ashon is not.

'He's half a breath from being tossed in for a swim with the hippos,' he drawls when Nico drifts off.

'Easy. At least he isn't calling me spotlight-hungry like a certain someone's ex.'

One eyebrow quirks. 'Payback's a bit—?' he begins.

'Bit of karma,' I finish, teasing.

But Ashon doesn't laugh. His jaw ticks. The next second he grabs my waist, hauls me flush against him and kisses me full on the mouth. It's slow and thorough and impossible to misunderstand.

The reeds rustle, a fish splashes, Nico mutters an awkward excuse and pivots to film the scenery.

When Ashon finally frees my lips, I'm breathing like I ran the length of the delta. 'W-what,' I whisper, 'was that for?'

He shrugs a broad shoulder. 'Claim staking.' His voice is gravel and smoke. Brazen as fire.

I roll my eyes but press closer. 'Primitive.'

'Effective,' he counters, his thumb stroking my lower back. 'But also possibly answers a few questions we both have.'

Head still spinning from last night and now this display, I wander ahead while he huddles with the crew, but I feel his gaze on me like a hot, possessive hand.

And I… I don't hate it.

Because it feels like the answer to Ashon's question is yes.

Yes.

CHAPTER NINE

Cilla

BY NOON WE'VE tromped through tall grass, mapped potential crane angles and picnicked beneath a fever tree. My feet ache and my cheeks hurt from grinning. Every so often Ashon leans in to murmur a thought about costume fabrics that breathe in heat, about a subplot where the 1950s heroine smuggles cocoa beans instead of diamonds. Each whisper feels conspiratorial, intimate, a private frequency only we share.

And beneath it all, my body thrums with the memory of his mouth on mine and the slow glide of skin on skin in the dark villa bedroom. I keep catching my reflection in the water and seeing a woman lightly sun-kissed, wholly satisfied and a little bit terrified of how much more she wants.

Back at the camp dock, Nico disembarks first, then Mpho starts the engine. Ashon helps me aboard last, lingering as the others turn away.

'You okay?' he asks quietly.

'Better than.' I bite my lip. 'This morning was…good.'

He studies me, resolve gleaming in his eyes again. 'But… or unexpectedly?'

'Unexpectedly,' I reply, not caring if it makes me weak or vulnerable.

Ashon nods, not disguising his smug pleasure. 'I meant what I said—about wanting you on the project.'

'Professional me or wife me?'

'Yes,' he murmurs, infuriatingly and sexily, and kisses my knuckles.

Heat unfurls in my stomach.

And later, as insects sing electrical choruses, I bathe, slip into a soft cotton nightdress and stand by the open screen watching fireflies spark over the floodplain. For the first time since this masquerade began, I feel…still.

Unperturbed. Maybe even bordering on…content?

Maybe I don't have to decide anything yet.

I promised a year. It's barely been weeks.

I can let the tide carry me for a while, savour the unexpected connection, the work, the baby's quiet flutter beneath my palm.

And yes, the sublime sex.

For now, can I accept the status quo? Wife, potential collaborator, possible wildcard in his script.

The truth whispering through my pulse is simple. Today felt like the start of something worth staying for.

And tomorrow?

Tomorrow I'll decide how brave I want to be.

One month later
Accra

The heat in Accra hits differently after you've breathed delta air and slept beneath Botswana stars, but it still feels like a promise. *Like...home.*

I pad across the marble floor of our new penthouse—yes, *our* penthouse—in the Airport residential area, a mug of milky rooibos warming my palms.

Twenty-one stories below, the city is murmuring awake. Hawkers calling *waakye* and traffic horns tuning up like brass bands.

One month since Botswana, and somehow everything has shifted without collapsing.

It's magic and mundane at once.

The magic? I'm sleeping with my husband—no, *making love* to him, though the hopeless romantic in me still winces at the phrasing. Blame pregnancy hormones or his sudden obsession with touching me every time I cross a room. Either way, the sex is sublime. Slow, thorough, sometimes so tender it terrifies me. He talks to my belly afterward, low promises I pretend to ignore while my heart cartwheels.

And sometimes when we're out at one of the many events, he showers me with delicious compliments. Like the one last night, when we met with his cousin Theo, who it turns out is the main architect for Ashon's studio project.

Theo had looked me up and down after brushing kisses on my cheeks. 'Pregnancy becomes you,' he'd said.

To which Ashon replied, 'Indeed it does. Motherhood will become her even better.'

My heart had tripped over several times, barely waiting for Theo to leave—after a curiously terse inquiry about Tessa my cousin—before I turned to my husband. 'And how do you know that?'

His gaze had met mine with unnerving intensity. 'Besides your feverish conversations you have with our child when you think no one's listening? Because I see how you fight for what you want, Cilla. You're built for motherhood the same way you're built for war. With everything you have.'

Of course that had robbed me of speech. Continued to wreak havoc with my emotions.

The excitingly mundane? I'm editing mood boards and

treatment decks at the breakfast counter like a half-hired consultant.

'Semi-professional,' Ashon tosses out, though the email I received from my agent regarding how much Ashon's studio plans to pay me for said work, made my jaw drop.

Best of all and, yes, I hate myself a little for my breathlessness when it happens, he actually *listens* when I say the third-act twist needs a female POV.

I allow myself a little smile after a sip of rooibos.

Convincing Ashon to leave Nana's fortress took one spectacular post-midnight session, a tangle of limbs on those ridiculous Frette sheets, my mouth still swollen when I whispered, *'Wouldn't it be nice to wake up and step outside without your grandfather's portrait scowling at us?'*

He groaned something obscene, half-annoyed that I'd summoned his grandfather into our discourse.

And yet, within forty-eight hours we were enroute across the city, with suitcases and a disgruntled Renée trailing logistics via FaceTime while grumbling about time zones and inhumane working conditions.

Now the walls around us are ours…well until decisions—*mine*—are made.

Soft sage, charcoal, framed production stills leaning casually while we argue about where to hang them. There's a nursery cornered off the master suite already painted a hopeful moonlit blue.

It should be perfect.

Except…

I can't get the echoes of the conversations with my mother out of my head. She's taken to calling every Sunday and, without fail, our video calls crescendo into scolding.

I still don't understand why you did this.

I raised you better than to chase a Biney man.

Have you forgotten why we lost the farm?

Marriage is not reparation, Priscilla.

I reassure her, show her the healthy-baby scan, promise a full explanation soon, but guilt blooms like bruises under my ribs.

Another fly in the otherwise clear ointment?

Each time I ease the conversation towards the land—*Have your lawyers heard from Nana's team? Any timeline?*—he kisses the question off my lips, or suggests gelato runs, or flat-out changes the subject.

Something isn't right. I feel it in the way his shoulders tense whenever my phone buzzes with Mom's name.

I pass my hand over the tight swell of my lower belly. I swore I wouldn't bury my head in the sand, but life feels dangerously sweet: sunrise sex, script meetings, baby flutters like tiny, secret drumbeats. Digging for answers means risking this equilibrium.

But…how long can I keep pretending I don't notice the rougher gravel in Ashon's voice when past and future legacy come up?

At first, I tell myself it's anything else but continued *deliberate* delays.

That contrary to what the registrar loftily states, the land transfer is complicated. Legal channels. Documentation. Verification.

But I also remember Botswana. And talk of plot twists and changing parameters. All of which seems to have been placed on ice since our return. I hate that I can't seem to gather the courage to reignite that conversation.

Because I'm terrified of an adverse outcome? That I would rather hang all of his…uncertainty on a piece of land.

I tell myself that's what started this and that I owe it to my family to see it through.

I recite it like a prayer. Like a woman trying not to admit she might have made the same mistake twice.

But by the end of the second week after our return, it's beginning to feel hollow, a snag I keep pulling at instead of cutting off. And when the legal assistant who once answered my emails in seconds now sends polite delays, I know I'm letting the prayer become a knot in my throat.

Ashon's still busy being the Biney heir. Hosting meetings. Touring potential locations. Rebranding himself as a Hollywood king who's come home to build an empire.

Sometimes I catch him on the phone at midnight, pacing the expansive terrace, shirt off, cool in direct defiance of the heat, barking orders in a low, dangerous voice. The same voice he used the night he bent me over the edge of his bed, called me sweet and sinful and his.

I stand on the back balcony one afternoon, sipping lemon water, press a hand to the spot just under my navel and remind myself that I am not the naive girl who cried herself to sleep over broken promises. Not any more.

But when I turn back into the penthouse, my reflection in the French doors says otherwise.

There's a distance growing between us.

And it isn't emotional. It's tactical.

Ashon

All good things come to an end...

Except I can't help but feel this particular end is entirely of my own doing. That a single act will reverse the carnage I can sense approaching. But...damn it, I can't help but lay blame either way.

So I keep silent on her land deed.

And she watches me like she's waiting for the lie to fall from my mouth.

And I hate it.

Hate how much I want her to believe in me. Hate how I notice when her dresses start to flow looser, when her hand drifts instinctively to her stomach but the joy is muted, how she still wears the ring but never plays with it.

The land.

I should have signed the documents by now.

They sit on my desk, ready. All that remains is a signature and a call to the family registrar.

But I haven't done it.

Because the timing is too perfect. Because as much as Botswana was sublime, possibly even a pathway to renegotiating something…more… I've heard her conversations with her mother. And now I can't tell if Cilla's presence in my life is fate or a move on a very long, very strategic chessboard.

She got pregnant. She agreed to the wedding. She asked for the land. I know all of that. But I also know there's a shoe waiting to drop. And for the first time in my life, I can't summon the balls to hasten that action. Besides withholding this last thing she wants.

What if she's just smarter than all the others?

I remember the story my grandfather told me when I was fifteen. Of a woman he loved who nearly cost him the family legacy. Of how she sweet-talked her way into deeds and influence before revealing she was a spy for their rivals.

He never forgave her. Never forgave himself either.

Echoes of Delphine, lingering in the shadows as a warning.

Are you sure?

Teeth gritted and yes, perhaps even mildly disgusted with myself, I summon Nana Biney's voice.

'Guard your inheritance,' he told me. 'Even from the ones who say they love you.'

I didn't think I'd carry that warning into my marriage.

But here I am.

Cilla

The answer arrives sooner than I want and entirely uninvited.

When the doorbell chimes, I expect the butler to bring in groceries or to usher in the designer commissioned with the wardrobe racks for tomorrow's promo shoot. Instead, the concierge accompanied by the butler, hands me a thick courier envelope addressed to Mr and Mrs Biney—Nana's law firm seal in heavy gold emboss.

My pulse stutters. I tear it open.

Inside is an executed deed transfer, decades old, signed over to the Biney Trust. The land's cadastral map is unmistakable—my parents' cocoa farm. Stamped *FINAL* in red.

But the date of final signature: one month ago. While we were in Botswana. And even worse? The thing that sends me sagging into the sofa, my breaths short and my visions hazing. The new owner of the land that belongs to me—Ashon Kobina Biney.

I should feel vindicated that fierce guarding of my emotions has been fully justified.

But I can't. Not when my stomach drops, nausea and betrayal roiling harder than first-trimester morning sickness ever did.

Muted voices sound, then hurried footsteps behind me.

I whirl. Ashon stands in the doorway, phone in hand, expression already tight—like he knows exactly what I'm holding.

So. The equilibrium ends here.

And I realise that sand isn't strong enough to hide the heads buried in them, not for ever, and especially not when the tide keeps rising.

Because all you risk then is drowning.

So I recite my most fervent prayer as my husband approaches. As the deed trembles in my grip.

I don't bother with prevarications. 'You knew,' I say, voice thin as cracked glass. 'You knew the land was finalised weeks ago and you didn't—'

'Cilla,' his voice is a warning. No surprise there, but there's a flash of something in his eyes. Something resembling an… imploration. 'You need to let me ex—'

'Explain?' A ragged laugh tears free. 'You've been stalling for weeks. How long did you expect to string me along for? The whole year? And then what, you were going to find some reason to explain away why my family's land is no longer your grandfather's but yours instead of—'

A sharp, hot spasm knifes low in my abdomen. I suck in air as the papers slip out of my hands, unheeded. As my palm splays across the small swell beneath my shirt.

No. *Oh God, no!*

Ashon's expression snaps from guarded to sharp to… *terrified*. 'Cilla. What's wrong?'

'I—don't know. It hurts.' Another cramp twists, fiercer. My heart drops and I cling to the arms of the chair, my knuckles screaming in pain.

Just as a slick warmth blooms between my thighs.

'Ashon! Oh God!'

In two lunges, he scoops me up. 'Silas, car—now!' he barks his stride already devouring the hallway.

Two hours later

Monitors beep in lazy, unwanted rhythms.

Antiseptic hangs in the chilled air and I swear to the heavens that if I never see another hospital, it'll be soon enough.

I lie on the narrow bed while a kindly obstetrician finishes an ultrasound sweep.

Time suspends in the air. Tension screams as we wait. Wait. *Wait.*

Ashon's fingers are tight around mine. And I allow it. For now.

'Good heartbeat,' she announces an eternity later, turning the screen so we both see the rhythmic flicker. 'No placental abruption, just mild cervical spotting—common at this stage. But you…' she adds with a stern look, directed at me, then at Ashon, as if she knows, '…need to rest. No stress.'

'Are you sure?' My voice is a hoarse, weak mess. 'About the heartbeat?'

Sympathy washes over her face and she turns the monitor to face us once more, redirecting the wand onto my belly. Once again the heartbeat echoes, louder than the other monitors. *Whoosh, whoosh, whoosh.*

I feel Ashon shudder with the same relief coursing through me. So hard I almost sob. And I do quietly in the hanky suddenly pushed into my hand, as she lists more cautionary measures.

'We'll keep you in for forty-eight hours for observation.'

Ashon exhales beside the bed, shoulders caving before he straightens, slipping the mask back on.

When the doctor leaves, silence swells—thick, unfinished.

He reaches for my hand. I let him—for now.

'I was going to tell you tonight,' he says, voice rough.

I laugh, a caustic sound that scrapes my throat. 'Very convenient, isn't it? When you could've mentioned it at the other two dozen dinners or breakfasts.' My throat is raw, equal parts fear and anger. 'And I'm sure you have an explanation as to why it's in your name rather than mine?'

'Because I didn't want Nana and his lawyers questioning why and getting in my way. Do I need to remind you that this is still supposed to be a love match? Do you really think divulging that the family of the woman I just so happen to be marrying used to own a portion of the very land I'm inheriting won't throw up a dozen red flags? I wanted to present it with the new trust documents—everything that proves it's yours again.' He drags a hand through his hair. The words hover, scented with truth and omission. Part of me wants to believe him; the other part remembers the cold stamp *FINAL*.

'Or you wanted to use it as leverage for whatever it is you want down the line from me.'

Something hard and rigid flashes over his face but with a trace of emotion I would call guilt if I didn't know better. 'I think we've established that trust isn't a thing I embrace very quickly, but, Cilla—'

'You're right. Which is why I don't know whether I can trust anything you say now, Ashon.' I whisper the harsh, unwanted truth.

He rears back, his eyes blackening. That flash returns, stays two seconds longer. Then his nostrils thin as he inhales long and deep.

He steps back from the bed and prowls to the window overlooking the sterile car park. For an eternity, we stay locked in our own hellish scenes.

His shoulders stiffen, in that way that tells me to brace myself.

'Very well, if that's how you feel…' he pauses, eyes shining with something close to resignation. 'Rest.' His eyes swing to the monitor. 'Keep our child safe. That's what matters right now.'

I close my eyes, exhaustion rolling over me. *Safe.* The word has edges I no longer recognise. But the baby's steady heartbeat still echoes in my ears, an anchor against the storm.

Forty-eight hours.

Two sleepless nights.

Plenty of time to decide what safety, and truth, really look like.

Ashon lowers himself into the visitor's chair, legs crossed, arms folded, an ocean away across the room. And slowly, slowly, his face closes off.

Outside the ward window, Accra's dusk gathers, violet and uncertain.

Waiting for the next act.

Ashon

My wife, who might no longer wish for the title, sleeps fitfully behind a glass door, her pulse line blinking steady green, but my heart refuses to match the rhythm.

Every rustle of a nurse's shoe makes my veins chill.

Every muted alarm farther down the ward punches fear through my ribs.

I'm going out of my damn mind.

Securing my legacy had felt like triumph, proof I'd finally out-manoeuvred Nana, secured the studio of my dreams, honoured my father. Now they feel radioactive. One glaring stamped date mark and the woman I'm trying not to lose was bleeding on our penthouse floor.

Cause and effect? The rational part of me says no. The superstitious boy still hiding under my skin isn't so sure.

I press knuckles to my forehead, replaying every excuse.

I'll tell her tonight.

She deserves the whole picture.

Just wait until the timing's right.

The timing is never right.

My grandfather weaponised time and used it against me until I bowed to his will, engaging in a fake relationship that's as far from fake now as the sun is from the moon.

I swore I'd be different, yet here I am, watching my cause and effect detonate before my eyes.

A wave of memory blindsides me—my father's hand on mine, his voice hoarse—*Legacy means nothing if the people you love can't share it.*

I was twenty-one, affronted over one thing or another and too angry to listen. Now his words vibrate like prophecy.

I stalk to the vending alcove, swipe a card I don't remember pulling out, and stare at rows of ginger biscuits she might stomach tomorrow. My hands shake. Anger, caffeine, terror—who the hell knows any more?

Footsteps. Renée. Of course she flew in the second she read my text.

'A CEO pacing a maternity wing at midnight is a bad look,' she says quietly, snatching the sofa and handing me water.

'What if I'm the bad look?' I mutter. 'What if I got everything I wanted and still lose her?'

Renée studies me, eyes soft but unyielding. 'Then fight harder. Not for deeds. For her. If she's what…who you want. Or are you arrogant enough not to admit that?'

My lips twitch. 'Arrogant is all well and good. But it doesn't keep me warm.'

'Then reclaim what does.' She nods towards Cilla's room. 'No time like the present. You taught me that.'

I turn, attempting and failing to ignore the dread and hope tangling in my throat.

Inside, she's propped against pillows, her eyes shut. I suspect she's not really asleep but pretending.

I cross to her, take her hand—warm, steady—and I grit my teeth. 'We'll have to talk about this sooner or later. We both know that.'

Without opening her eyes, she turns away. 'Maybe. But not tonight. Tonight I can't stand to look at you.'

'Be that as it may, I intend to look at you. I have to. Because I simply cannot.'

All truth, shockingly raw and scraping every inch of my chest, I retreat to my chair for my harrowing vigil.

Because certain other truths are locking into place. I suspect I delayed and prevaricated because of a greater purpose.

Which is that when it comes right down to it, the land means nothing. The studio is hollow. And legacy—mine, Nana's, all of it—is just empty acreage without the woman who turned my façade into a life.

Of course I can't confess all of that now. It'll be a hollow, desperate reaction of my unravelling world.

Still, my heart leaps when she cracks her beautiful eyes open. Except what I see, uncertainty and fury flickering there, but also something fragile I pray isn't finished, rocks me to my core.

So it's a good thing I'm sitting down.

I stare at my wife, the woman who owns a far greater chunk of me than I bargained for, and I breathe in the antiseptic night…until she falls asleep.

Cilla

True to his word, and much to my traitor heart's delight, Ashon moves closer while I'm asleep and plants himself beside the bed like a sentry, tension radiating off him in brutal, silent waves. His thumbs drum the railing. His answers when doctors and nurses float in are calm, clipped and precise, each syllable weighted with warning and prime expectation.

But not when he addresses me.

'Water?' he asks, a distinct gentleness in his voice.

I shake my head. 'No thanks, I'm fine.'

'The doctor was pleased with the latest scan.'

'I know. She told me.'

A beat. His jaw ticks. 'Need anything else?'

'Yes,' I whisper. 'An explanation,' I say, voice hoarse. 'Why is Renée camped outside my room? Shouldn't the great Ashon Biney's right hand be in LA greasing palms and green-lighting sequels? Or hunched over blueprints with Theo.'

He shakes his head. 'Theo can handle my requirements without me looking over his shoulder. And Renée's here because she's worried—about you, about us.'

'Right,' I scoff. 'She just flew halfway around the world to hold my coconut water.'

A quirked eyebrow greets my caustic response. 'Since you're evidently feeling feisty…' he says in a drawl tone, '…shall we clear the air?'

'Sure,' I whisper. 'Tell me the ways you intend to re-establish the baseline trust you've broken.'

He exhales through his nose. 'I told you, it—' He scrubs a hand over his face. 'The timing was—'

'Convenient,' I finish. 'For you.'

He paces three steps, pivots. 'You want a confession? Yes, I handled it wrong. I was trying to stage it—'

'Like a scene in one of your movies.' My voice cracks. 'I'm not a set piece, Ashon.'

Silence expands, thick as plaster. Finally he says, 'This is going nowhere. Rest. We'll talk when you're stronger.'

'I'm strong enough now.' The monitor beeps faster. 'Much stronger than you think.'

He flinches at the spike, then nudges his head at the monitor. 'No, you're not. I won't have you distressed again. If you won't do it for me, do it for the baby, Cilla.'

Weariness floods me, heavy as lead. I close my eyes. 'Fine. I need sleep. Go home.'

His jaw ripples. 'There won't be many times you will get away with sending me away—'

'Then I'll make hay now, thanks. Go away, Ashon.'

After a terse little moment where his gleaming eyes promise retribution, he picks up my hand, presses a kiss to my knuckles and then walks out, tension rigid in every line of him.

As victories go, it's an inconsequential one because, of course, I miss his presence the second he leaves. And when the door swings open again what feels like minutes later, I assume he's back. To torment and overwhelm. To remind me that my heart is on the steep decline to betraying me.

But it's not my husband who walks through the doors.

It's… Nana.

Impeccable Kente, gold-handled walking cane, smile carved in polished stone.

'Child,' he murmurs, feigned warmth coating every syllable. 'I came as soon as I heard.'

I clutch the sheet to my chest. 'How magnanimous. A phone call would've sufficed.'

He chuckles, pulling a chair closer. 'Grandchildren are a blessing. Great-grandchildren even more so. But some blessings must be earned.' He looks around. 'And it looks like you're being tested as to whether you deserve yours.'

I say nothing, probably because of the fury and anguish fighting for supremacy within me.

After several beats, he raises an eyebrow. 'Nothing to say?'

I summon a starched smile. 'It looks like you're on a roll, Nana. And far be it for me to interrupt my elder.'

He smiles in return but it looks as brittle and disingenuous as I feel. 'While you and my grandson enjoyed your honeymoon safari and scouting, I did a bit of scouting of my own.' His smile sharpens. 'Interesting history. Loans unpaid. Land forfeited. Painful, yes—but all above board.'

My pulse pounds. 'Only if you deem extreme coercion *above board*.'

'And now you intend to right that historical inconvenience?' He taps his cane once. 'Revenge is a…dangerous hobby for expectant mothers.'

My throat tightens. 'I want what was stolen. That's all.'

'That's *not* all.' His gaze hardens. 'You want a seat at my table. You want to rewrite the Biney name.' He leans closer, voice a scalpel. 'Understand me, girl. If you push this, I will raze what remains of your family's reputation. No more fancy documentaries for you. No more cushy tenure for your uncle.' He shakes his head. 'Choose wisely, girl. Let what's left of the Rocksons live their lives in peace.'

A tremor shudders through me, equal parts fury and fear. 'And Ashon?'

'I build heirs,' he says, rising. 'I do not let them be led by ambition-mad wives. He knows his place. You will learn yours.'

He straightens his *ntoma*, mask of concern snapping back in place. 'Rest well. Stress is unkind to babies.' With that, he glides out, cane tapping like a countdown.

The door clicks shut.

The tears come hot and unstoppable with anger, betrayal,

terror for the child who twists gently inside me as if asking what storm we've walked into.

I reach for the call button, then drop my hand.

Nana and his grandson have spies everywhere. I need a little more quiet. Peace.

But first I need a plan. One that protects my baby, my family, and—if I'm honest—the man who might break with his grandfather for my child…break *me* to keep what he believes to be his.

CHAPTER TEN

Ashon

I'M HALFWAY OUT of a production call when Renée's message lands.

Nana just left the hospital. Did you know he was visiting your wife?

Ice sluices through my veins and for once I'm thankful for the pomposity of a motorcade that allows me to cut through traffic.

The SUV barely stops before I'm in motion. I don't bother with waiting for busy elevators—four flights taken two at a time gets me where I need to be.

And in the last few seconds before I burst into the private wing, lungs burning, I'm abashed by the notion that I'm rushing to protect my wife from…*my grandfather*?

Sure, he wasn't entirely happy when we announced we would be moving out of his house and immediate influence but do I really fear for her?

Or is this more terror of not making a bad situation I've created, worse? Of still being hesitant to admit the heaviest emotion to myself for fear of…of—

Cilla's room is dim and quiet, but the air inside is charged, heavy with everything unspoken. She sits propped against the pillows, arms crossed, face blotched with dried tears. But the moment she sees me, she swipes a wrist across her cheek and lifts her chin, armour snapping into place like she's prepping for war.

'I know he was here. What did he say to you?' My voice is hoarse, ragged with twisted emotions I barely keep leashed.

She doesn't flinch. 'What do you think? More Biney threats, more tossing about his power and might on people he deems smaller than him. Confirmation that trust is a fragile thing, especially when it's misplaced.'

I grit my teeth at the anguish and fury in her voice. 'Cilla, there's nothing he can say that'll make a difference to you and I. You know that, don't you?' I'm aware I'm being vague, that damn stranglehold keeping me prisoner, which is ironic because vivid expression has been my mainstay, making me a billionaire long before I turned thirty.

She searches my gaze for a tight minute, probably looking for the same clarity before she shakes her head. 'I don't care. I'm leaving, Ashon. As soon as I'm cleared to fly, I'm going back to the States.'

A low throb ignites at the base of my skull. 'Just so we're clear, by the States you mean Los Angeles, correct?'

Her mouth works for a moment. 'I guess you'll find out, won't you.'

My insides clench with steel knots. 'Not fucking good enough, I'm afraid, wife. You're not leaving me. Not with our agreement in place. Not with my child still in your womb.'

Her brows rise, slow and cool. 'We can come to another arrangement—later. After the baby's born.'

'What arrangement?' I step closer. 'You call in for joint custody over FaceTime? Send postcards from Nebraska or Montana or some other place that isn't where I am? That wasn't the deal.'

'Deals change,' she snaps. 'Especially when threats start flying from the lips of your family patriarch.'

'What did he say?' I repeat, harder, harsher than before. 'I'm going to find out one way or the other so you might as well spill it.'

She meets my gaze squarely. 'That he'll destroy what's left of the Rocksons if I don't back off the land claim. That he "builds heirs" and doesn't let them be led by ambition-mad wives.' The laughter she tacks on has 'as if' written all over it.

And a sheet of shock goes through me, because it's clear this woman doesn't know her true power. That over and above the precious child she carries, my every other breath is fast-encroaching obsession levels where she's concerned.

My hands curl into fists. I don't even know I'm pacing until I hear my footsteps echo off the sterile tiles. 'So that's it?' I snarl. 'You run? Let him win?'

'I'm not running. I'm surviving. That's what people like me do.'

'People like you?' My laugh is hollow. 'What does that mean?'

She lifts her chin higher. 'It means I can't afford to be part of your legacy soap opera. I knew the role I was playing. Botswana was a good script,' she says quietly, eyes darting away. 'Exceptional, even. But it was just make-believe.'

The words slice deeper than I expect. I reel from it, and I know she sees it because her face softens, regret catching in her expression. 'Wasn't it?' she probes, a little more vulnerable now. 'Tell me I'm wrong.'

I want to. God, I want to. But the words wedge in my throat.

So I do what I've always done. I pivot.

'Maybe it was. Maybe you're right,' I say, my voice flatter than I feel. 'So here's the new third-act rewrite. You're moving into my house in Bel-Air. We leave only after the doctors clear you and a medical team is on my jet. Non-negotiable.'

She stares at me, hollow-eyed, and for the first time I think she sees me not as a man but as the machinery of empire I was born into.

After a long silence, she nods. 'Fine.'

I don't know if it's victory or failure. I move to the edge of the bed, but I don't sit. My knuckles ache from clenching. My mind is a whirlwind.

Would my father have done this? Something cringes and dies inside me.

No. My father believed in freedom. In partnership. He never tried to dominate people no matter their status. And wasn't that what he always said? *Love without freedom is just control in disguise.*

And here I am. Disguising.

But I can't let her go. Can't risk her being across the ocean where I can't reach her. Not when everything inside me is already halfway unravelled.

And somewhere deep inside, I hear my father's voice. *Don't become the thing your grandfather used to break me.*

I want to promise I won't.

But I don't know if I can keep that promise.

As she lies back, too weary to hold the anger any more, I brush a damp curl from her temple. She doesn't flinch. Doesn't meet my eyes.

And that might be the worst part of all.

As she drifts into uneasy sleep, I wonder which of us I've condemned by doing this.

Her?

Or me?

Cilla

The Bel-Air mansion hasn't changed, but I have.

It's a strange, almost cruel symmetry, returning not as the

help but as the wife. Not in a uniform, but in soft designer loungewear tailored to my swelling belly, carrying a child I never imagined would tie me so irrevocably to the man I once planned to forget.

I move through the foyer like a ghost retracing old steps. The place is pristine, cold, curated to the point of sterility. Ashon's taste, or maybe Renée's. Nothing of me here, except the bottles of my preferred shampoo in the guest suite he had prepared right next to his.

No, most likely not prepared. *Commandeered.*

'My apartment in Koreatown…' I say the moment I find him in the kitchen, casually sipping from a crystal tumbler like he's not just rewritten my life. 'I need to go and get my things.'

He doesn't even flinch. 'No need. I've had everything moved. Your things are in the third guest suite upstairs. You can sort through what you want to keep or dispose of when you're stronger.'

My fingers curl around the edge of the island. 'You had no right to do that without my permission.'

'You're pregnant,' he says, deadpan. 'I didn't want you anywhere near that hovel lifting boxes or catching heavy things. It's done. Let's move on.'

I stare at him, every muscle taut. 'So now you bulldoze every choice I make in the name of faux care and attention?'

His jaw flexes. 'No. I bulldoze for you because I can. And because I care if you live in a shoebox with cracked tiles and a neighbour who argues with his dog.'

I blink. That…was not what I expected. But it doesn't soften me. I don't let it. 'Well. Maybe you should've told me,' I say. 'I might've even said thank you.'

A beat of silence. Then, 'I don't need your thanks.'

'No,' I whisper, turning away. 'Just my obedience.'

As I climb the stairs, I think about how, once upon a time, this man said he wished things could be like they were in Botswana. Simple. Joyful. Real.

And yet here we are back in the belly of the loathsome beast named hubris.

Upstairs, I find my belongings exactly where he said, arranged with precision. My books on documentaries. My film festival posters. Even my little worn-out notebook, set on the desk like it belongs. I should be grateful. But all I feel is… displaced.

When the laptop pings its familiar tone, I ignore it. Then curiosity and something more desperate gets the better of me.

Returning to my suite, I sit at my desk and open the email. I'm searching for a distraction but my heart is already racing a little because I know the distraction I'm searching for is specific. Something…anything to do with my husband.

It's from Renée.

RE: Obibini-Treatment Notes

I should reply to say I'm no longer part of the great Biney team. Or better yet, delete the email.

But I don't. My fingers hover, then move. I click it open.

It's a production update. Scene breakdowns. Notes from the writers. A section left blank with a highlighted comment:

Cilla's POV? She always sees the emotional arc others miss. Would love her input.

My heart thuds.

I haven't thought about the Obibini project since the hospital.

I told myself I can't afford to remain invested. Especially since I'd begun to imagine a future that didn't hinge on legacy, but on love. On this new family I wasn't anticipating but had kindled in Cap Ferrat and felt vastly possible in the fiery magic of Botswana.

But even before I can caution myself on the wisdom of it, I start to type.

Scene 27 works because it's raw. Because he doesn't trust her and she doesn't trust herself. And that tension—that ache—isn't about what they say, it's about what they don't.

My throat tightens as my fingers hover over the send button, and my eyes begin to sting and water.

This isn't just about a movie any more. Of course it isn't. It's about me. Him. *Us.*

I shake as I hit send. I should feel powerful. Vindicated that I'm rising above.

Instead, I feel exposed. Because if I care about the work this much… I care about him.

And if I care about him…

Breath shuddering out, I press my hand to the gentle curve of my stomach, now firm under my cashmere sweater.

I don't know if I'll ever get back those thousand acres for my family.

But I do know this. I *love* him, the man whose name represents my family's destruction. Who introduced me to this heightened feeling I doubt I'll ever be rid of. Who in a few short months will help introduce me to motherhood.

For good or ill, I've been falling in love with Ashon since Botswana. Maybe since Cap Ferrat. Or even right here, in this vast monument to his talent and power when I caught a glimpse of everything he is when all else is stripped away.

Heaven help me, I'm already there, quietly, entirely.

So now what?

Do I cling to the past? Or protect what's growing inside me, even if it means letting go of the past? Of what ignited all this?

My baby kicks—the strongest one yet, like a heartbeat I can feel within my palm.

Maybe the answer isn't one or the other.

Maybe it's finding the space in between.

And choosing something new. Something equally powerful.

Everlasting.

If I dare?

Ashon

The late-night office is quiet except for the soft rustle of script pages and the glow of my laptop. I'm half-listening to a producer drone about merchandising when an alert pops:

RE: Treatment Notes and Music Rights Proposal
From: Cilla Rockson
To: Renée cc: Ashon Biney

She should be asleep, is my first thought.

My second act is to glance up, as if I've achieved x-ray ability to see through walls to the woman who's brazenly avoiding me.

My third, an eager attempt to devour anything to do with my wife is to click on the email.

A three-line reply, but it's pure Cilla—crisp, insightful, a reference to that South African composer we discovered on a veranda in Botswana while in post-coital bliss.

Heat pools in my loins at the memory while higher, in my chest and the place I'm still reluctant to examine, a deeper warmth collects.

If she hasn't checked out of my professional life—not completely—then maybe she hasn't checked out of *us*.

If it's not too late, then act quickly.

Teeth setting and chest thumping, I start a measured, appreciative answer, nothing needy, when another ping slices the moment.

Subject: URGENT—Land Inquiry
From: Nana's Legal Counsel
To: Ashon Biney
Cc: Nana Biney
Attached: Preliminary Legal Action Over Rockson Family Parcel—Central Region.
Claimants: The Rockson Family.

Nana's note atop the thread: *'She never stops scheming.'*

Ice floods my veins. The inquiry is two weeks old, demanding copies of all documents to the land. The request isn't signed by Cilla, it's her cousin Tessa's, but the letterhead bears her contact details, her address, her phone number.

Did she know?

Is this why she stayed?

I'm out of the office before the thought finishes, barefoot, righteous fury and something I refuse to admit is fear tangling inside my throat. Right alongside it is the very convenient thought that I was right to wait. To assess. Because this proves I was right to. Doesn't it?

Upstairs, in the media room, she's curled on a sofa in one of my threadbare hoodies, bare legs tucked under her. She looks up—peaceful turning to wary as she sees my face.

'Cilla.'

Her fingers pluck at the hem of the hoodie, as if she's contemplating taking it off now I've seen her in it. 'What's wrong?'

I thrust the computer at her. 'Explain this.'

She skims the document, then her shoulders sag. 'That's my cousin. She's over-protective.'

'But she used your name.'

'It's family, Ashon. They meddle. You of all people should know that. And they meddle harder when you don't have answers for them because your husband is keeping secrets.'

I ignore the sting for something more imperative. Something that feels like my whole life is hinging on it. Is it entirely unfair? Maybe. But all is fair in love and war, isn't it? 'That inquiry's two weeks old. Right after Botswana.'

Her eyes widen, confusion giving way to pain she immediately tries to hide with pride and affront. 'You think I filed that?'

'Why not? You played house, charmed me, fucked me, then accused me of subterfuge—who wouldn't suspect?'

Tears glint but don't fall. 'You bastard! I was trying to l—' She freezes. As do I.

Her lips tremble. A thousand unspoken things flash in her eyes.

But she shuts them tight like that'll help cage the truth.

'Say it,' I murmur, gentler now. 'To what, Cilla?'

She flinches like I've slapped her. Then silence swells between us, thick as wet clay. Smothering and reshaping and destroying.

'Say what this is really about. Because it stopped being about land a long time ago.'

Her eyes fly open. 'Oh no,' she says, voice cracking. 'You don't get to root around for something you don't deserve. You don't get to hold all your cards to your chest, Ashon. I'm *so damn tired* of pretending I'm the only one who feels something here while you just wait in the wings for me to fuck up.'

I suck in a breath that burns going down because, God, isn't there a boat load of truth in there? This harrowing sensation of the shoe about to drop? Or has it dropped already and I'm too blind to see it?

She doesn't move.

Neither do I.

But I can't. I just…can't say the words pounding at the back of my throat.

Not when admitting it would break open everything I've spent my whole life trying to keep locked up.

Her laugh is short. Shaky. Heartbreaking. 'You can't even give me scraps, can you?' she whispers. 'Not even now. I thought you'd be man enough, but clearly, I was wrong.'

More silence throbs.

I open my mouth to answer the taunt, but it's too late.

She draws herself up, pain morphing to armour. 'Then let's end this farce while I still have some pride left.'

'Cilla—'

'No! Get out,' she says, the words quiet but lethal. 'Leave me the hell alone.'

I retreat—backwards through the hallway, down the stairs, into darkness that suddenly feels far more honest than the light I just destroyed.

Cilla

Ashon's footsteps stalk down the hallway, fast and purposeful, as if he can't stand another second inside the same walls. The front door slams a moment later. Silence billows out to fill the space he leaves behind. It's so loud I hear the pulse in my neck.

I stare at the email on the laptop he thrust into my hands.

My cousin Tessa's digital signature.

My name in the 'beneficiary' line.

My phone number. My address.

Proof, if you're looking for it, that I'm still the Rockson girl clawing for restitution.

I'm so tired of proof. Of everyone demanding it emotionally and physically. Of me trying to contain and outrun it.

A single tear slides, hot and humiliating, before I swipe it away and shove to my feet. The hoodie—his hoodie—hangs to my mid-thigh, smelling of sandalwood and yearning—*mine.* I peel it off as if it scorches me, toss it over the back of the couch, and pad upstairs to the guest suite he curated like a personal museum of my old life.

The room feels suddenly alien. My stack of books here, the Sundance lanyard neatly pinned to a corkboard propped on the floor over there. Artefacts of a woman who believed justice could be bought with patience and a heart filled with inherited righteousness.

I feel like a robot when I pull a small roller suitcase from the closet. I don't need much. Laptop, camera, pre-natals, that foolish dream-notebook of documentary pitches.

The baby kicks, soft and inquisitive when I bend to pack shirts. 'It's okay,' I whisper, though my throat burns. 'We'll land on our feet. We always do.'

I hesitate over the envelope of new ultrasound photos. Botswana feels so distant now, like a film I once screened and then misplaced the reel. I tuck the images into my purse anyway. Some memories are worth keeping even if they hurt.

Phone and purse and charger.

Done.

When my phone rings my heart jumps, until I remember Ashon stormed out, is unlikely to call. A quick glance at the screen and I'm not sure I'm relieved or anxious that my mother has chosen this moment to ring, as if the universe needs witnesses to my undoing.

I answer on the second buzz, forcing steadiness. 'Hi, Ma?'

'What's wrong? You sound winded,' she says. 'Everything all right?'

I close my eyes. 'Yes…no… I don't know.'

A sigh crackles over the line, equal parts worry and judgement. 'Cilla, come home. Whatever that man promised, he's still a Biney.'

'He promised me nothing tonight.' My voice breaks on the last word.

Silence. Then softer: 'Child, loving a powerful man is a dangerous game. Make sure you hold all the pieces before you play.'

I want to argue, explain how he touched my belly, how he laughed with me over morogo stew in the delta, how he whispered *plot twist* like a vow. But all I say is, 'Thanks, Ma. I'll call you soon.'

Suitcase packed, I roll it down the landing. Halfway to the stairs I freeze.

The nursery door, the small room between guest suite and master—sits ajar. I toured it when we first arrived but not since, not being in the state of mind to start picking baby blankets and booties.

But someone has clearly been in there, putting furniture together while I wasn't paying attention.

Ashon?

My heart leaps into my throat as I step inside.

Turn in a full circle. A white crib, plush giraffe, a tiny Biney-blue blanket with pink flowers embroidered with *Baby Biney.*

My heart cleaves. No matter how furious I am, the sight of that blanket wrecks me.

I step in, fingertips brushing the crib rail. There's a note taped to the mobile:

'Record your lullabies here.'

Below is a voice-memo mic and a flash-drive already labelled *Cilla's Songs*.

The ache and the yearning are instant, raw.

Am I holding an overblown grudge?

Maybe he never told me about the deeds because he wanted some grand reveal, like Cap Ferrat sunsets and Botswana stars. Maybe he's just a man who doesn't know how to lead with vulnerability, so he leads with strategy.

But strategy pulverised my parents. He knew that. And he allowed it to pulverise me.

The window of benefit of the doubt has been left open too long. I can't help but remember that moment in the hospital when I hoped…*prayed* he would echo what lurked in my heart.

He didn't.

It's time to close the window.

I wheel the suitcase to the foyer.

The rideshare confirmation demand blinks in my phone, but my thumb hovers.

If I leave now, I cut the last thread. No more Mrs Biney, no more front-row seats to the raw and reckless beauty of his dreams, no more Ashon, the man who kisses me like I'm the centre of a universe he alone can create.

I'd be walking away from the laughter that curls out of him at midnight, the rough velvet of his promises against my skin, the way his eyes soften when our baby's heartbeat echoes in a quiet room.

But I meant what I said. I can't stand in this overwhelming emotion alone, and he…he's not ready to stand with me.

I'm not sure the emptiness that follows would hurt any less than staying.

But those were pockets of wonder borrowed from time, fleeting sparks that can't outshine the shadows settling in our cracks, and I'm terrified that once they fade, all I'll have left is the echo of what might have been.

A sob climbs my chest. I clamp a hand over my mouth and head for the door.

Just as headlights slash the driveway. Did I hit the ride-share button by accident?

I check my phone. No, I didn't.

So it can only be…

I hear the roar of Ashon's sports car before I see it. He's back already?

Panic spikes. I can't face him. Not like this.

I duck behind the curve of the staircase just as the door opens, then hightail it for the kitchen.

Ashon's voice, low, rough and wrecked, floats through the foyer. 'Renée, she'll be heading for the airport. Have security intercept her. Get her on the jet, make sure she doesn't exert herself. No, I don't care what it costs. She wants distance, give her the Gulfstream. But make sure a doctor's on board.'

A heavy breath. 'And call Tessa Rockson. Tell her if she meddles again, I'll—' He breaks off, voice splintering. 'No. Forget it. Just… I'll call her myself. This mess is my creation. I'll fix it.'

My pulse stutters. He's not scheming—he's scrambling. Problem solving. Making amends the only way he knows how. For me.

In that instant the floor seems to tilt. I thought power was his language, but maybe his real dialect is *control as apology.* And maybe he's terrified because he knows control is the one currency I won't accept any more.

I straighten, rolling the suitcase back away from the kitchen, deeper into the house instead of the door. A new plan buds, clearer, braver. If we're going to rewrite this script, it has to start with a scene the audience never sees coming.

I square my shoulders and head down the hall to face the man who breaks things trying to save them—and decide if love is worth letting him try again.

I linger behind the wide staircase, suitcase in hand, listening to Ashon's ragged half-orders swirl through the marble foyer. One part of me wants to bolt—cling to outrage the way a drowning woman clings to driftwood. Another part aches at the cracks in his voice, the way he stumbles over threats he can't bring himself to finish.

He's scared, a small voice whispers. *And hurt. All of this has hurt him too.*

But fear doesn't erase the stranglehold of his control, does it? It doesn't return years of my parents' dignity.

I retreat into a pool of moonlight by the tall windows, pulse thudding. Outside, the jasmine hedge is heavy with white blossoms, their scent drifting through the open transom like a memory of Botswana nights—of laughter, of trust that felt almost real.

Is it foolish to miss that feeling? To want it back?

I think of my mother's brittle pride the day our farm title vanished. The tremble in my father's hands every time he opened another rejection letter. I promised restitution, reclaiming what was ours. *Justice, Cilla. Not romance.* The vow has defined me for so long I'm not sure who I am without its iron edge.

Yet here I stand, heart twisting at the sound of my husband's broken breathing.

What if justice can live alongside love?

What if the greatest victory isn't wresting land from the

Biney empire, but forging a future where our child never has to choose between the two surnames stitched into their blood?

I rub my belly, feel a soft flurry, our little one responding to the storm inside me.

A tear slips, warm against my cheek. I want to build a home that isn't balanced on revenge. A story that isn't written in spite.

But wanting that means trusting Ashon—and trusting myself to temper his power, not be devoured by it. Am I strong enough?

Footsteps approach. I swipe at my face and step from the shadows before he can find me cowering. His eyes widen, a mixture of relief and exhaustion and…*hope?* So raw it pierces me.

Neither of us speaks.

I set the suitcase down gently. His gaze drops to it, then back to me, more haunted than I've ever seen it. 'I thought you'd be long gone by now.' He glances down at his phone. 'I was waiting to hear how far you'd decided you need to be away from me this time.'

The lump grows in my throat. 'I know,' I whisper. 'It…it took me longer than I thought to pack.' A short, hard laugh escapes my throat. 'I keep packing the past like it can travel with me. Maybe I should spare myself the burden of hauling ghosts and the past around.'

He swallows hard. 'I booked the jet because I thought…if distance is what you need—'

'What I need…' I interrupt, pulse racing, '…is truth. No more power plays. No more withholding. I need to know you see me—my family's story, my dreams—as more than leverage. I need to know that you…feel something. For me. *Just me.*'

He steps closer, anguish flickering across his face. 'I don't just see you, Cilla. You're all I see and it terrifies me because I only know how to fight for goals, then set them free. I'm not used to… I don't know how to cherish the things that remain. The things that claw their way into my soul.'

Silence stretches. The jasmine scent thickens, mingling with the salt of my unshed tears.

'If we stay,' I say slowly, 'it has to be a new script. Signed by both of us.'

'Co-written,' he murmurs hoarsely.

'Co-directed,' I add, a wobbly smile teasing my lips.

His answering smile is faint, trembling at the corners—like the sun breaking through harmattan haze. 'Then rewrite it with me.'

For the first time I let myself believe we might. But belief isn't enough. Action must follow.

The baby kicks. A decision knocks quietly into place inside my heart. Maybe legacy isn't what you inherit. Maybe it's what you choose to build together after the wreckage.

I extend my hand. He takes it, his thumb stroking the pulse at my wrist.

The internal debate quiets, soothed by possibility. Tomorrow could break us all over again. But tonight I choose the risk. I choose him. I choose us.

And as he drapes his hoodie back around my shoulders, I realise something staggering. For the first time, justice and love don't feel mutually exclusive. They feel—miraculously—like the same fight.

CHAPTER ELEVEN

Ashon

IT FEELS LIKE a lot was said but not nearly enough. As though we laid down the first fragile bricks of a bridge and then stepped back, still staring at the chasm.

I've begun the slow machinery of righting wrongs, yet the final act—whether it turns out to be the sword of Damocles poised above my marriage or the crowning triumph of my life—still hovers just beyond reach, humming with expectation.

Dawn finds me in the Bel-Air bedroom, sunlight slicing across the rug like a harsh spotlight that records every restless mile I've paced through the night.

Cilla's finally drifted into a light, exhausted sleep, curled beneath my hoodie—another one that she seemed to be able to locate and help herself to without my knowing. An accidental banner of truce that makes my chest ache with hope and fear in equal measure.

But I know too well that words murmured in a moon-washed foyer are only fragile intentions, and intentions without swift, tangible action are precisely how my family has twisted promises into weapons for generations.

I cannot—*will not*—let that be our story.

So I move before the sun is fully awake.

At precisely 6:03 a.m. my voice, raw from sleeplessness, rasps into the phone as I call my vastly overpriced lawyers. An emergency meeting is set at ten, the Rockson file, the irrevocable non-profit template we used to honour my father—yes, *irrevocable*, I stress, because this time there must be no loophole, no retreat, no reversal.

I instruct them to draft a deed that sends the Central Region farm—every centimetre of soil, every cocoa tree, every memory—straight into a newly minted Rockson Trust. A foundation bearing her parents' names, Kwesi and Adjoa, because their descendants, including our child, deserve to stand eternal alongside whatever monuments the Bineys build going forward.

I barely hang up before dialling Renée, who answers on the first ring, loyal and ever awake. The woman deserves the obscene bonus coming her way this Christmas.

I tell her I want a twenty-four-hour press blackout, total radio silence. No leaks about Obibini, no breath of gossip about the marriage that half of Hollywood still thinks is a convenient headline.

She pauses, this woman who knows me almost too well. 'What's going on? Cilla never arrived at the airport. Since you're not panicking I'm assuming you know where she is?'

I glance into the living room, at the breathtaking woman curled up on the sofa.

The woman who owns my heart, soul and everything in between. 'Yes, I do.'

A soft sigh of relief. 'So what's happening then? Are we in damage-control mode again?'

'No,' I whisper because the word tastes wrong. 'Redemption mode.' The admission scrapes my throat, but it feels like truth for the first time in days.

Months, even.

By nine o'clock I'm planted at the head of Mason and Okoye's glass boardroom—an aquarium of LA skyline and polished intimidation—glowering at a semicircle of junior partners who look like they'd rather face a firing squad than my impatience.

'Show me the Rockson file,' I bark, snapping my fingers.

A paralegal slides a leather folder across the table.

I flip it open, skimming final deeds, trust certificates, a glossy prospectus titled *The Kwesi & Adjoa Rockson Foundation*—her parents' names foiled in gold.

Good start. But the knot inside doesn't ease one iota.

'Sir,' the senior partner ventures, throat tight, 'the foundation charter you requested is fully irrevocable. Once your wife signs, you relinquish all control.'

'That's the point,' I cut in. 'Power belongs to her now. Cross-check every clause, then courier these to my house by noon.' I tap the cover once, hard. 'I want the world to know a Biney can give without expecting tribute.'

Silence. Then a collective rustle of 'Understood, Mr Biney.'

I lean back, voice dropping. 'And include the memorandum for the Koforidua farming incubator. Seed money, half a million to start—annual top-ups indexed for inflation.'

A junior lawyer blinks. 'That fast?'

'"Fast" is the only speed that fixes what I broke.'

And fast is how I return to her, luckily avoiding being stopped for speeding.

Back home the house is hushed, sunlight spilling through atrium windows.

I know Cilla's around because I have access to the cameras, I've seen her moving around, spending most of her time in the kitchen, peeling another mango with the kind of nostalgia that makes my heart ache and makes me vow to repeat a thousand of those scenes in the decades to come.

Climbing the stairs I enter the nursery first, to make a few more promises, then I knock on her door.

She doesn't answer, but the door swings open to reveal my sleeping, pregnant wife.

Crossing the room, I stare at her, the sleeping woman I love more than anything or anyone else in this world.

I lay the foundation folder on her dressing table, then sit at her desk and scribble a note on thick ivory stationery.

My hand trembles as I add a final line, a promise I've never put in ink.

I tuck the note under the pen she used to sign our first bogus contract. Then I press a kiss to her sleeping forehead and a gentle hand to her belly—linger long enough to feel the soft flutter of our child between us—and step back.

Cilla

The first thing I see when my eyelids flutter open is a leather folder propped against my pillow like a waiting sentinel. The second—far more arresting, heart-stopping—is a single folded sheet of ivory stationery resting on top.

Instinct tells me my future doesn't live inside the embossed file but inside that scrap of paper, that whatever it contains will either stitch the torn edges of my heart or slice them wider. My fingers tremble as I reach, hesitation snagging each breath until I finally unfold it.

Ashon's handwriting—hard, masculine, unapologetic—fills the page.

Cilla,
I was wrong and paper alone can't say it.

The land is yours, the foundation in your parents' names.

I know I need several takes to earn your trust.

Be the exceptional wife you've been, the generous and loving mother you're destined to become, and grant me just one more?

I beg of you.

—Ashon

PS—No more hidden scenes, only the story we write together.

Even before I finish the first line, tears blur the ink. The note smells faintly of his cologne—sandalwood and, deliberate or unintended, it makes my heart fuller.

It feels like an olive branch, a confession and an invocation all at once.

My pulse hammers as I slip from the bed, clutching the folder and note to my chest. Sunlight spills in soft stripes across polished hardwood, guiding me down the hall to the nursery where my instincts guide me.

And there he is, a king of my heart, of my very being, even kneeling on the carpet with a tiny onesie draped over his broad hands, a picture of hope and contrition I never expected to see on a Biney face. A picture that doesn't in any way diminish him, but makes him human.

Mine, please God.

He lifts his head and the emotion in his eyes is so raw I stop breathing. Suspicion rises first—I've learned survival the hard way—but it's chased quickly by a flutter of fragile hope.

'I owe you more than an apology,' he begins, voice low and rough, like gravel softened by rain. 'The deepest apology. I owe you the truth I kept and the land that was never mine to sign.'

He extends another thick envelope with my parents' names gleaming in gold script across the top. I don't take it, not yet.

Instead I search his face with what I hope is clinical calm. But how can calm exist when love is beating wild beneath my ribs?

'It's all yours,' he continues, the words reverent. 'The whole site. Irrevocable. Today. Your parents guiding every seed planted.' He swallows visibly.

My hands tremble and leather folder slips, unheeded, to the floor. 'What? Why? I never wanted this…more than what was taken. This is your legacy, what's you've worked all your life for.'

'Because withholding it, even it was out of fear that without it you wouldn't stay with me, that you would end our marriage, only made me Nana Biney's grandson, not my father's son. Dad fought for people, not property. His refusal to bow down to Nana's control took its toll on him but he was never a prisoner. He lived free. I thought I'd emulated him, but it turned out I only went so far and not far enough. I regressed into the wrong Biney when I fought to hold onto you in the wrong way.'

He starts to write but shakes his head and sinks back onto one knee. Something inside me buckles. Ashon Biney—Bel-Air titan, red-carpet monarch—dropping into supplication for me.

'I can't fix the past…' he says, voice cracking on the admission, '…but I can promise a future built on equal footing. I love you, Cilla Rockson-Biney—every fierce, brilliant, stubborn inch of you. I love our child.' His trembling palm settles over the gentle swell of my belly, as though he's making a vow directly to the tiny heartbeat inside. 'And I love the version of me that only exists when you're in the room. Please…rewrite the story with me.'

I let out a shaky, half-sobbing laugh, one that tastes of tears and hope tangled together. 'No, Ashon, I want to burn the old script and start brand-new.'

'Then we start now,' he murmurs, leaning his forehead against mine, breath unsteady. 'No secret drafts. Every scene, every line, out in the open.' He draws a ragged breath, smile wobbling but undeniable and unapologetic. Raw and beautiful as only he can be, this man of my heart. 'I'll spend the rest of my life proving the new ending is worth the pain of every earlier take.'

'And I'll hold you to it,' I whisper, covering his hand with mine. 'Solid promise?'

'Solid gold,' he vows, voice low but certain. 'As long as there's breath in me, you'll never question where you stand in my story again.'

Between us, our baby gives a tiny kick, an unspoken cue that this, finally, is the scene it was waiting to join.

Hot tears blur my vision.

I set the letter aside and finally open the envelope. I skim read it because I trust but my heart catches all the same. 'You'd really give up a thirty-million-dollar project for me?' My voice wavers between awe and disbelief.

'For *us*. For what's right. For what love looks like when I'm not afraid.' His answer is immediate, unflinching.

Silence grows, fills with the scent of talc and jasmine.

I lower myself to the rug opposite him, knees nearly touching. I cup his jaw, feel the tremor in his stubble-rough cheeks.

'Then my answer is yes, to everything, but especially to the man who finally led with his heart.'

He breaks—actually breaks—into a shuddering breath he's probably been holding for years. I kiss him, salt and jasmine, and the papers slip to the floor while our arms wrap tightly around a future we were almost too blind to see.

'Tell me, my love, but only if you think I've earned it,' he whispers against my mouth, the mouth I'm yearning for him to kiss.

'And if you haven't?' I tease because I can. Because hope and love and the promise of forever is heady enough, freeing enough, to let me.

'Then I'll working tirelessly. Day and night for it.'

I drop my forehead to his, breathe him in. Then, 'I love you, Ashon. So much I can't bear a moment when I have to take a breath without the power of it fuelling me. I love you. I love you. *I love you.*'

A shudder rips through him, through me, and then we're both breaking again, him into grateful sobs, me into a breath that sounds like release after years underwater.

We collapse onto the soft carpet, desperately clutching each other. Above us, the mobile our baby will enjoy spins tiny felt elephants dancing in lazy circles.

I envision that very scene while the love of my life whispers deep, heartfelt promises in my ear.

And for the first time since this torrid, impossible story began, every scene feels exposed to sunlight. No hidden takes, just the raw, uncut reel of two hearts choosing to trust again.

Ashon

I follow her up the polished stairwell, my pulse pounding like it did the very first night she climbed those Bel-Air steps, then as my housekeeper, now as my wife, always as my undoing.

Bedroom doors swing shut behind us with a muted click and the city outside recedes to a shimmer of distant lights.

She turns, hair spilling over her shoulders, the curve of her belly framed in moon wash. 'Last chance, Mr Biney. Walk away if legacy means more than this.' Her challenge is pure fire, but her eyes are soft, brimming with the love she finally let herself confess.

I cross the floor in two strides, gather her close. 'Legacy?'

I whisper against her mouth. 'Legacy is right here.' I kiss her slow, savouring the tremble that ripples through her when my tongue brushes hers. My hands glide over warm skin, relearning every path, the slope of her waist, the swell of her breasts, the fluttering life beneath my palm. She moans into my mouth, hips angling for closer contact, a silent dare.

Clothing falls away—hers first, then mine—until skin meets skin and the air itself feels electrified. I lay her back on crisp linen, half-worship, half-reverence, tracing the faint silver at her hips, proof of the miracle we created.

She arches impatiently, fingers tunnelling into my hair, guiding my mouth down the column of her throat.

We find a rhythm that feels both brand-new and achingly familiar, bodies gliding in a dance refined by every hard lesson we survived. Her nails bite my shoulders, grounding me and I murmur promises against her skin.

When she finally shatters beneath me, crying out my name like a benediction, I tumble after her, the rush obliterating every doubt I ever harboured.

Breathless, we lie tangled, hearts racing in unison. I brush damp hair from her forehead and she answers with that luminous, sleepy smile that always unthreads me.

'I'll accept your gift on one condition,' she whispers, her voice still velvet from pleasure. 'You carry through with your original dream for that land—build the first Obibini studio there, a place where African stories are filmed by African actors for the whole world to see.'

I frown. 'Cilla, you don't have to. I can find somewhere else—'

'No, you won't. That's my condition remember?'

'Are you sure, my love?'

'With every bone in my body.'

'And what a beautiful body it is,' I growl, kissing her hard, then soft, then groaning because this feeling…it's exceptional in every way. And I'm still floored it's mine.

'I'll agree to your condition but only if you agree in turn that the foundation's film wing will fund young Ghanaian documentarians. And you'll curate.'

Her smile lights the world. And mine. 'Deal.'

The promise ignites in my chest like sunrise. 'Then we'll break ground together,' I swear, threading my fingers through hers. 'And every frame will carry your heartbeat.'

'Co-directed?'

I laugh, the sound bursting bright as sunlight after rain. 'Co-directed,' I echo our midnight vow.

Chimes from the hallway clock fade as she rises, my fertile goddess, belly swollen with our child, naked and undeniably mine, hips swaying towards the door. 'Where are you going?' I call, fascinated.

'Follow me and you'll find out.'

Downstairs the kitchen glows under soft pendant lights. She selects a fat mango from the pantry, slices it open, juice glistening on her fingers. I lick the sweetness from her wrist, cannot resist tasting more. The fruit tumbles forgotten as we end up against the counter, kissing sticky laughter into each other's mouths.

I lift her onto the cool marble, enter her slow and deep, a shiver of moans and groans and eternity at our very fingertips.

We make love again with only devotion sealed in whispered *I-love-you's*.

Much later, as she drifts to sleep on my chest, I breathe a silent prayer to my father. The man whose compass I almost failed to follow. The man I know would be proud I managed to salvage this.

Legacy secured, Da, but not the way Nana meant. A better way—her way—our way.

For once, the weight of the Biney name feels like wings instead of chains.

Tomorrow we'll tell the world.

Tonight, in the hush of our bedroom and the steady beat of two hearts finally in sync, I know the story's last act has begun, and it's a love story, after all.

EPILOGUE

Ashon

THE VAST LAWN of the new Obibini Studios proposed compound shimmers under late-afternoon sun, awash in blinding white parasols and the low thrum of Afrobeats music.

I can feel the ground vibrate with expectation—our guests, the press, the whole of Africa's creative scene waiting to baptise this place with applause—and yet every sound seems to muffle when I look at my wife.

Reporters crowd the step-and-repeat we had flown in from Paris, camera flashes popping like restless fireflies, but their lenses keep sliding in our direction.

They can't help it. No one can when Cilla's in the frame.

She stands in a jewel-green sheath that kisses every curve motherhood left behind, her braids woven into a coronet that gleams beneath the sun. Cradled against her heart in a butter-yellow wrap is Amélia Afua Biney, our twelve-week-old miracle, already surveying the world with the same toffee-dark eyes that once brought Hollywood executives to heel.

God, I'm helpless in the presence of these two women.

I adjust the baby's blanket, brushing a kiss over Cilla's temple. 'You're luminous,' I whisper. 'If I were a sane man I'd keep you hidden, but the world deserves to see what real royalty looks like.'

She tips her head back, offers me that half-moon smile that still wrecks my pulse. 'Behave, Mr Biney. You have a kingdom to dedicate.'

I should be nervous, but her confidence buoys me. I turn and notice Nana's gilt chair—empty, conspicuously so—but the old man's absence feels like freedom, not a hollow space. Tonight belongs to our daughter, to Cilla and to the stories we'll tell.

As I guide her through the crowd, we pause to greet family, industry giants and one or two strategically invited frenemies. But just before we step onto the platform, I notice Cilla's gaze snag on something—or someone—across the courtyard.

Her brows knit together. 'Is that…why is Theo glaring at Tessa?'

I glance over. Sure enough, my cousin looks like he's been sucker-punched by the vision of her cousin in cobalt silk. And Tessa? She's pretending to be unmoved, but the fire in her eyes says otherwise.

Cilla leans in, voice low. 'Do you know what happened between them?'

I smirk. 'No. But that's their story to tell.'

When I stride to the podium, applause washes over me in warm waves. The giant screen behind freezes on the last frame of *Tides of Tomorrow*, the Botswana—Ghana docudrama Cilla midwifed into greatness.

Cannes hailed it, BAFTA short-listed it and I would trade every statuette for the glow on her cheeks right now.

I clear my throat and the crowd stills. Yeah, I might be humbled in many ways, but that never gets old.

'This studio began as a promise to my father—Kwame Biney—who taught me that stories outlive stone. Tonight, I dedicate our first film to him…and to the woman who taught me to fight for something greater than legacy.'

I turn to my wife, my compass. My everything.

'Cilla, every frame carries your courage. Every note of the score echoes your heartbeat. Thank you for giving our daughter a world where love and justice share the same screen.'

Flashbulbs flare, but my gaze never leaves hers.

She lifts trembling fingertips to her lips, pride and tenderness blazing brighter than the spotlights. In that look, I read the whole journey: Bel-Air, Cap Ferrat, Botswana, heartbreak, forgiveness and the future refused to surrender.

Hours later the city sighs itself to sleep, interrupted by the faintest horn blasts even at this time. Moonlight pours silver across the nursery's pastel walls. Amélia breathes to soft lullabies from her bassinet while Cilla smooths her blanket, gentler than dawn.

I lean in the doorway, arms folded, reverence lodged in my throat. Two strides and she's in my arms, jasmine warmth and quiet triumph moulding to my chest.

'I never believed in fate until you,' I murmur, letting the words vibrate against her ear. 'I didn't know what home was until I found it in your arms.'

She shivers, my steel-spined warrior undone by a sentence. 'Say it again.'

I frame her face, memorising every eyelash. 'I love you, Cilla Rockson-Biney. More than land, more than legacy, more than every red-carpet dream I ever chased.'

Her answer is a kiss, soft, then luxuriously deep, a signature in ink and sighs across my soul. A tiny foot thumps muslin, Amélia's sleepy kick feels like applause.

Cilla laughs into my mouth, breath warm. 'Our critic approves.'

'Smart girl.' I nibble her lower lip, hunger curling low. 'She understands the best films always earn a sequel.' I slide a palm to her waist, then lower, feeling her melt against me. 'What would you say, Mrs Biney, if her daddy asked for another co-production?'

Heat flickers in her eyes, a sunset I want to drown in. She leans up, brushes her mouth along my jaw, voice coy. 'I might already be ahead of you, Mr Biney.'

My heart stalls, then soars. 'You're— Are you?'

She presses a finger to my lips. 'Tomorrow's story. Tonight, just hold me.'

We sway by the bassinet, moonlight painting our silhouettes into one.

Outside, Accra's night hums on, unaware that inside this quiet room a legacy far richer than trophies or acreage has rooted itself—growing, kicking and multiplying.

And as her cheek rests over my heartbeat, I vow that every sequel we create—on screen or in life—will be co-directed, co-written and bathed in the same unstoppable light that began with a single, reckless kiss.

* * * * *

If you just couldn't get enough of
Vengeance to Baby Vows,
then be sure to check out the next instalment in the
Billionaires in the Spotlight duet, coming soon!
And why not explore these other stories by Maya Blake?

Enemy's Game of Revenge
Crowned for His Son
Out of Office Nights
Snowbound and Royally Forbidden
Keeping a Greek Secret

Available now!